High Fyelds

A NEW BEGINNING

SEVEN OF STARS

Also by Mae McKinnon

HIGH FYELDS – THE BIG RACE
Seven of Stars

MAGICAL MISCHIEF – A MOTIONBOOK
Seven of Stars

THE DAMSEL AND THE DRAGON
Seven of Stars

ACADEMIA DRACONIA
Seven of Stars

DAWN OF THE WINDS
(credited as M. Aei)
Seven of Stars

WOLF'S BANE
(credited as M. Aei)
Seven of Stars

High Fyelds

A NEW BEGINNING

SEVEN OF STARS

Mae McKinnon

DRAGONQUILL PUBLISHING

High Fyelds – A New Beginning
A DragonQuill book

Cover art and logo by Juliane Völker
nightpark-art.de

Cover design by Marlene Ockersse

Formatting by Marlene Ockersse

Edited by Ashley Lachance
scribecat.ca

First Printed in France, 2018

ISBN: 978-91-983535-9-4
A CIP catalogue record for this book is available from the National Library of Sweden

DragonQuill Publishing
www.dragonquillpublishing.wordpress.com

CHAPTERS

CHAPTER ONE 7

CHAPTER TWO 12

CHAPTER THREE..23

CHAPTER FOUR 33

CHAPTER FIVE 47

CHAPTER SIX 60

CHAPTER SEVEN..68

CHAPTER EIGHT..75

CHAPTER NINE...86

CHAPTER TEN 92

Acknowledgements 108

Chrono-order of the Seven of Stars Novels.........................109

AD 110

This one's for the Muse.
It's a rascally thing that lives on tea and dreams,
and travels the worlds in the blink of an eye.

One day, I hope it invites me along …

CHAPTER ONE

In the time-honoured method of emergency repairs everywhere, Erina hit the console in front of her with her fists.

'Stop. Stop! STOP!' she screamed at it.

It didn't help much, but at least it served as a release for her pent-up frustration. Plus, she'd already tried everything else.

The shuttlecraft didn't take much notice. Shaking violently, it skirted the upper atmosphere of the planet like a pebble thrown across the water by a very poorly-sighted giant. They weren't the type of pebble that would sink calmly to the bottom of the pond but were, judging by their luck so far, going to end up as a scattered and very hot debris field, somewhere. Not much of a comparison at all when you thought of it like that.

Around her, the normally so soothing hum of the engines had been replaced by crackles, hissing and spitting across the walls and ceiling, from the various electronics.

In the passenger compartment behind her, everyone was getting strapped in. Nearly everyone. One was trying, desperately, to put out the flames leaping from one of the panels. The passenger struggled against the violent swinging motions of the shuttle, holding on to the extinguisher with one hand and the seatback with another.

With everything rocking from side to side, the internal inertial dampeners were struggling to compensate for the wild descent. It was also possible that they'd actually stopped working and the only thing that kept them all from dropping, like a very nicely designed proverbial rock, were the wings.

Maybe they hadn't worked properly since they'd hit that asteroid. This would, actually, explain a lot.

Risking a look out of the starboard viewport, Erina watched those bits of metal and plastasteele (or whatever it was that you built these things out of, goodness knew she wasn't a mechanic) threatening to be pulled out of their sockets as the ship skimmed the upper atmosphere.

The engines shorted out, dropping them into the churning storm below with all the grace of a lump of granite.

They all screamed as their stomachs hit their gullets. Blood drained from their skulls in momentary terror. Then, with a nasal whine, the power returned. The engines kicked back in. A semblance of control was restored.

It probably wouldn't last long. Erina was almost glad she couldn't see much but swirling damp greyness as the clouds buffered them this way, then that. Almost anything was better than seeing the ground rushing up to meet you, she thought.

The yoke in her hands was trembling, fighting her as she tried to keep them steady. Normally, the computer interpreted your instructions, transmitting them to every part of the ship for easy navigation and a smooth journey. Normally, it took a delicate touch even if the controls of the shuttle weren't as sensitive as those of the starfighters she was used to. Now she was wrestling it, forcing every twist and turn to be executed by sheer will.

Mostly, it was all she could do to stop them spinning wildly out of control.

Turned out that hitting that asteroid had been a very bad move. Hah. Who would have thought? That the autopilot probably *"hadn't meant too"* didn't make it any less of a nuisance. It was just one of those things that happened. She just wished it wasn't happening to *her*.

'DO something!' one of the passengers yelled at her from behind.

'Like what? Sprout wings?' Erina shouted back.

The noise around them was deafening. Rolls of thunder boomed through the shuttle, making their ears ring and pop at the same time. Static electricity leapt over the control boards, stinging anything it touched.

A frazzle erupted from the nearby coms unit. The tendrils of smoke it emitted tasted bitter, scratching at their throats even before they could see it.

'Great. Just frigging great,' Erina snarled at the machine. She couldn't take her hands off the yoke to deal with it. Her head was spinning. She'd bit her tongue earlier, the hot taste of iron now dripping down her chin.

It wasn't the first time she'd flown something that got into trouble. But, usually, the only one she had to worry about was herself. Now, she risked a glance behind her. Her passengers didn't look any happier than she was. Several of them were clamping their eyes shut. All of them were holding on to their seats as if their life depended on it, fingers whitening.

This wouldn't have happened at all if she'd had a ship of her own, Erina was sure of that. That ship would have had all sorts of modifications. It certainly *wouldn't* have had an autopilot stupid enough to set a course right through several hundred tons of ice and rock.

'Watch out!' someone screamed.

The cry was enough that Erina's attention snapped back to where they were going.

Something swooshed past them. Gone too fast for her to make out, it thudded on the hull. Bouncing against it several times, it left behind … was that *feathers*? Yes. There were feathers stuck on her windscreen.

At this altitude? But that was impossible. Wasn't it?

'What the rach was that?' Josh called out.

'How should I know?' Erina snapped back.

Whatever the feathers had been attached to, it had moved out of the way on its own accord. The large, dark shadow looming where it had been, didn't. It stood, steady as a rock.

It should. It *was* a rock. In fact, it was the summit of a mountain.

There should have been tens of thousands of feet between them and the flat mixture of sea and desert that made up the ground around here.

Ok, so it was a very, *very* tall mountain.

That didn't explain what it was doing here. And it still wasn't moving.

'Oh, bugger!' Erina exclaimed.

Judging from the shouts coming from behind her, she wasn't the only one caught off guard. 'Pull up. PULL UP!' they all screamed.

'What the hell do you think I'm *trying* to do?'

Several billion tons of mountain was probably *not* up for a game of chicken, Erina thought, pulling at the yoke with all her strength.

The shuttle banked with agonizing slowness, screaming in protest.

'Was that a bloody mountain?'

'Don't be ridiculous. We're way above the stratosphere. There's no mountains up here.'

'Then what the frak did we almost hit?'

'SHUT UP back there!' Erina barked at her passengers. The world was swimming before her eyes. She didn't need them distracting her, too.

Wings trembling from the turbulence, the shuttle broke out of the cloudbank and screamed across mountainside's thick with snow and stone.

Two fins tore apart as they hit a snow bank, turning their world white. They burst through it, bounced into the air again as the engines fired one last time, and shot over a craggy ridge.

A pointed carpet met them below. Forests. Giant conifers climbing the mountainside, reaching for the stars, frozen in ice.

They dropped, again and again. Downwards, the shuttle headed. Ever downwards. It was shaking madly now. The air, usually so soft and pliable, had turned into the slap of a giant, knocking them this way, then that, as the pressure grew.

Wrestling back even a semblance of control felt almost impossible. They spun out, still screaming, as Erina managed to get the shuttle level enough just in time to avoid hitting another, lesser, peak.

Losing altitude fast now, they shot over the soft greens of leafy forests, rolling hills and plains of emerald grass, where they sent herds of fine-limbed creatures scattering in all directions.

'Almost down now,' Erina breathed. 'Almost. Just a little more.'

Then, as if rising out of the mist like a huge wave, came another line of trees. Another forest.

'Fire! Blast them!' someone shouted through the din.

'What d'you think this is? A starfighter? We don't HAVE any weapons!' Erina yelled, clenching her teeth. The pit in her stomach was tightening. She could practically taste the sweat in the air. The fear.

They were too low. Crowns of leaf and bark scraped their belly. Banging against the hull, tree after tree tore their gnarly fingers into the shuttle. It was like being inside a tin can repeatedly struck by rocks. Or a listing freighter, slowly creaking as it fell over on its side and crushed everything beneath it with agonising metallic moans — only sped up about a hundred times.

Ten minutes ago they would have torn through it, leaving nothing standing but burning stumps. But their speed had slowed. Were they going too fast? Or too slow? What was the optimum speed at which to crash? Was there one?

'Everyone! HOLD ON!' Erina shouted through the bedlam.

Down in the valley, some of the inhabitants briefly lifted their heads, moist eyes following the flaming balls of fire as more loose debris streaked into the shuttle's wake.

Less than a couple of heartbeats later, the noise and burning smoke disappeared beyond the hills, setting some of them aflame as it passed.

Alert ears flickered nervously. Then, when any immediate threat failed to emerge, their owners returned to grazing.

The shuttle slammed into the ground with the almighty noise of broken dreams. The earth was anything but soft and the shuttle scattered plating, stabilizers, and fuselage, as it ploughed through the soil.

Huge clumps of mud and grass were torn up and tossed aside like paper in the wind.

Slowing, almost as if against its will, the torn wreckage eventually came to a stop on the outskirts of an almost flat plain. Behind it, the trail of broken trees ended abruptly.

Then, it just lay there. The hot metal of the hull pinged as it cooled. Smoke spiralled, almost lazily, into the pristine air.

As if it had held its breath, around them, the sounds of the world returned. But, from the shuttle, there was silence.

CHAPTER TWO

C hatter. Indistinct chatter. Murmurs from beyond a veil of nothingness. It wasn't audible. Not really. She could feel the sounds rather than hear them. But somehow, they weren't quite right.

Something else drifted into her awareness from far away. From very, *very* far away. It pounded unmercifully on the door of her consciousness. Cookies. Cookies, it said. No. Wookies. Wakies? Wake. Wake up. That was it. It was telling her to, 'Wake. Up!'

Go away. Erina's unconscious mind shoved hard. We're warm and snug and pleasantly curled up right where we are. We know all about that *other* place. It's cold and dripping and full of people making all sorts of demands on time we can spend in better company — like our own — so thank you. But no thank you. Shoo. Shoo!

Smacking her lips as she drifted from unconsciousness to sleep, Erina tried to shut out the increasingly nasal whine. She didn't want to wake up. She was warm and snug. The ship could do without her for another snooze or two. It wasn't going to fall apart just because she wasn't there. It wasn't as if she was the captain or anything.

Just five more minutes, Erina dreamed hazily.

'Please wake up!' the distant voice kept pleading.

Getting louder and louder, it sounded familiar ... vaguely so. Why did it sound familiar? What was anyone doing in her quarters anyway? She had most certainly locked the door. She always did. So how had they gotten in?

Suddenly wide awake, Erina rolled over. Tried to roll over. She was jolted by a sharp pain in her side. Why couldn't she move? Someone was going to pay dearly for this intrusion, she promised herself.

Wide awake but not quite aware of where she was, it took several moments for what had happened to begin drifting back.

For starters, this wasn't her quarters, Erina realized. So much for yawning and sleepily dragging herself to wash and dress.

'Well, isn't this going to be the bad start to a day,' she grumbled.

Her legs were stinging. Something had clearly crawled into her mouth and died — three days ago, judging by the taste.

Two amber eyes popped open. The world came flooding back to her. It wasn't nearly as pleasant as the shuttlecraft had been before they'd crashed. For starters, it was murky. She tried blinking away the stinging sensation in her eyes. It didn't help.

The only light drifted in from far behind her — must be daylight she decided — and a single emergency glow stick. Still, it was better than total darkness. At least, this way she could *see* the four feet of twisted metal bulkhead that was looking very threatening — especially the broken ends — at her side.

So, that was what she'd tried to roll on to. It was close enough to poke her, should she move too much.

Wincing, she tried pushing it aside. Lodged among the other contorted debris around, it creaked but didn't budge. Getting speared on that wouldn't have been a very nice experience, Erina decided.

'Suppose it's a good thing these held,' she said and tugged at the harness. Not usually one to bother with strapping in, the dishwasher antics of the shuttle had made even her put safety first.

Pulling the safety, the harness retracted, dropping her on to the floor. Well, a wall pretending to be a floor. It was the correct way a floor should be in her mind, below her.

It would have been nice if it had been smooth and flat to land on but no such luck. She jerked back when she stepped on something sticking out of the general debris. Scraping it off her boot, she flung it aside. Tiny as the piece of metal had been, it had hurt — a lot.

'Great. And here I thought my day couldn't get any worse,' Erina muttered darkly.

Ignoring the scrambling noises from further down, Erina stretched. Nothing seemed to be broken. But she was going to be sore for days, she just knew it. Even her bruises had bruises.

'Cognitor, praise the stars, thought you were a goner, for sure.'

Growling at this assault on her ears, Erina blinked away the last of her confusion. They'd crashed, hadn't they? As the descent had steepened, all their instruments had stopped working one after one.

So, exactly where were they? And why wasn't there a rescue team here already? They should have picked up their distress signals already back at the asteroid.

If Search & Rescue took their time to find them... Well, that was going to play merry hell with her schedule, that was for sure.

'I am NOT deaf,' she grunted as, slowly, she found some safe footing amongst the debris. Since much of what had come loose had collected on the wall/floor, this was easier said than done and she picked her way with care.

Everywhere ached. Places she didn't even know she had, ached. Were kneecaps supposed to throb?

'Last thing I remember, this stupid bucket of bolts was trying a new career as a washing-machine,' she complained to the world at large. 'Guess that didn't work out so well.'

''s'pp'se so,' the other human replied.

Erina squinted hard. It was difficult to make out any distinguishing features below the yellow mop.

Racking her brain desperately, rosters and orders drifted past her inner eye and, eventually, took a stab at a name to go along with the mop-bucket.

'Josh, right?'

'Yes m'm.'

'You start calling me "m'm" and I'll have your insides strewn out faster than you can say shish-kebab — which, incidentally, is about how I feel right now.'

'Umm, right m'— Err ... Cognitor?' Josh licked his lips nervously. He'd heard the stories. They all had.

Usually the job attracted calm, analytical people who could talk their way out of anything. When Erina had taken up the position on the *Random Star*, it had soon become obvious that "usual" was not the best word to describe her approach.

Climbing out of the wreckage, the suns shoved bright, glaring light into their eyes from a blue sky dotted with sheep.

Where had the storm gone? The size of that thing, it couldn't just have vanished? Now that she was thinking about it, the weather hadn't been causing a ruckus since their first run-in with the mountain. A fell, a cone, of snow thousands upon thousands of feet high. Snowfell. But there should still be traces of it on the sky, shouldn't there?

'Don't suppose you happened to see what we landed in, did you?' Erina asked. 'Looks like some sort of grassland with trees to me.'

Shading her eyes and ignoring the immediate area, which was liberally strewn with parts of the shuttle that hadn't, well, stayed attached to the actual ship, she could make out several vague outlines of mountains hidden behind a veil of sunmist. One particular one towered above the rest.

'That must be the one we almost hit,' she observed. 'Snowfell.'

'Lucky us.'

'That remains to be seen. Do *you* know where we are?'

'No m'… Cognitor.'

'Me neither. And, in my book, that's usually not a good thing.'

Tall that they may be, the other mountains were some distance away and if you didn't know they were there, they could have been mistaken for darker blobs of cloud. There seemed to be bits of forest closer by and, Erina squinted, they were leafy, airy even, out here on the edge.

We must be quite far down from where we hit the first time, she thought. Those trees had, essentially, been one heavy mass off needles scraping up and against each other, like an angry, single organism.

With some of the plants on this world, if you didn't know what to look for, it was hard to tell them apart from those of old Earth. Not that she'd ever seen the originals, apart from as pictures on her diom, the handy, portable computer that it was.

Even when the colonists had used seeds from old Earth, in the soil here some of them had taken on rather unexpected properties as they'd grown.

Facing the other way, there was nothing. Just grass, growing from anything that wasn't rock (and some things that were). She could make out some gentle hills in the distance and, at the very horizon, something jagged and pointy that could be another small mountain range.

What she could see was sky. Lots and lots of sky.

'I don't know about you, Josh; Casticia might be a sparsely populated planet, but I'm sure I would have remembered if there was a bloody, hundreds of miles high, bit of it sticking half-way out of the ruddy atmosphere.'

A slight tick twitched for a moment near her left eye. Erina took a deep breath — the air here smelled good, almost a bit peachy — and beat down her annoyance with a metaphorical slap.

'You sure we landed on the right planet, Cognitor?'

'Positive. Same one as we took off from. Kind of hard to miss at that distance really.'

A moment of silence and the mix of burnt metal and sweet grass mingled as they stood staring at the clouds above them.

'This is not how I imagined the sky would look from a mesa this high. And how can we be breathing? Where did all this,' she waved her hand about agitatedly, 'biology, come from?'

'I don't know, Cognitor.'

'Me neither. Isn't it going to be fun finding out?' Erina snorted and waved away her new companion's reply before he'd even had a chance to air it.

'There should be *some* sign of civilization, surely? Satellites? Space stations? They should be hard to miss at this altitude. Heck, I'm surprised some of them haven't crashed into the place already. Haven't you spotted *anything*?'

'No,' Josh shook his head. 'No visuals. No signals. Nothing.'

'Where the rach are we?' Erina kept querying the air as she strolled around the crash site, picking up pieces and throwing them away, seemingly at random.

For a moment, Josh wondered what she was doing. It didn't really serve a purpose. Then he kicked himself. He'd forgotten who he was dealing with.

'The moons are still there, Cognitor.'

'All of them?'

'Yes.'

'So, we didn't fall through a hole in space-time and end up somewhere else. That's nice to know.'

'Doesn't look like, m'm.'

'More importantly,' Erina's sharp voice drew him back to reality. 'Where is everyone else?'

'Dead, Cognitor.'

Erina digested this news with a shrug. 'You live, and then you don't,' she mused philosophically. Personally, she much preferred the first.

'No sign of a rescue either, I presume?'

'No signals, Cognitor, m'm. Can't do a thing without signals.'

'Don't suppose they read smoke signals,' Erina sighed. She glanced at the main wreckage. It looked like bits of it had burned quite extensively. It should have sent a plume high into the sky. So much for hoping they could leave quickly.

'How about you? All in one piece?' Erina asked, as she took stock of the situation. 'You're not a dead man walking, are you?'

'Yeah,' Josh answered affirmatively. 'No, I mean no ...' Confusion reigned on his face, then he held up his hands, hopelessly. 'Alive m'—Alive.'

'Guess that's something,' Erina said.

She stretched again, trying to get rid of some of the soreness in her muscles. Being stuck in that harness for goodness knew how long hadn't done her any favours. What she could really do with right now was a nice, hot bath. Yeah, that wasn't going to happen. This place didn't look like prime hot-springs country. And the shuttlecraft didn't have a shower even when it was in one piece.

She aimed a small kick at the shuttle's main body. Another piece of plating dropped off it.

'Shuttle's mostly wrecked. We're mostly not. Now what do we do?'

'Umm—'

'Rhetorical!' Erina sighed. 'Suppose this mess isn't going to sort itself out. We might as well hop to it.' And with that, she cracked her fingers and disappeared back into the wrecked craft.

It was going to take more than just tenacity to get them through this, she thought as she pushed random bits of debris aside. Where did all this stuff come from? At this rate, they were going to have more random weird bits of metal and circuitry than they had ever had ship. Either way, the shuttle sure as heck wasn't going to fly anywhere — except maybe in a hurricane.

Poking at the various instruments, mostly to see if they turned on or not —half the stuff she had no idea what they did — the shuttlecraft having been retrofitted as a science-station. For a moment, it looked like they'd lucked out. The communications console seemed to have survived intact.

The small noise of excitement drew in the only other human nearby. Sadly, no matter how or what they prodded it with, it refused to work. It might be in one piece, but it was just as dead as everything else around them.

Erina and Josh looked at each other.

'Do *you* know how to fix this?' they both asked in unison.

'I can *use* it,' Josh supplied, trying to be helpful.

'Wonderful,' Erina scoffed. 'That makes two of us.'

Eventually, they managed to locate the emergency gear somewhere in the general mess. It contained, amongst other things, a handheld emergency communicator.

Normally they'd just use their dioms, but those weren't working either right now.

Shaking it about, after first pushing every external button there was to push[1], Josh held it up to his ear.

'Can't 'ear a thing,' he said and handed it back to the Cognitor.

Erina tossed it over her shoulder. 'So much for the easy way out, eh? Let's see what else is in here.'

The kit contained the standards you'd have expected. Shelter. Rations. Some medical supplies. Minor utensils. Ultra blankets and so forth. It was a means to keep going, for a while.

They certainly wouldn't starve for some time as no one had been nibbling at the rations in the kit when they'd felt peckish and had forgotten to replace them (unlike the painkillers, half of which were already gone).

This said more about the taste of the *food* than anything else. You might

---

[1] One.

18

not want to chew off your own foot before you ate some, but you might consider boiling your footwear. Especially if you had nice, rach-hide boots.

Erina's hand unconsciously drifted down to hers. Even now they felt smooth against her calves. No, no way she was going to eat those. She chased away the thought.

No, they wouldn't starve and maybe they wouldn't freeze either — who knew how low the temperature dropped here at night — as, amongst their prizes, there turned up a portable heater.

A few minutes later, it was pushed aside with a disgusted huff.

'What is it with these confounded contraptions?' Erina snarled at the electronics, as the portable heater refused to fire.

'Maybe something here eats power?' Josh suggested. 'Look, the indicator says it's full. It's just not working.'

'Great. So now we're trapped in the Valley of the Lost with something that eats pow? Oh yes, that sounds really likely. There must be tons of pow around here for them to survive on when they can't munch on a crashed satellite or two,' Erina rolled her eyes theatrically. 'I don't suppose you're going to suggest we've crash landed into the middle of fairyland while you're at it?'

'You asked, Cognitor,' Josh replied, a little hurt.

'Right. So, basically, we're down to "roughing it" then? Just what I always wanted,' Erina snorted sarcastically, rolling her eyes again.

'But, you must have been to *all* the planets in the solar system? Even the frontier ones.'

'*And* most of the moons. Doesn't mean I *like* living under domes, below the ground or floating around in cities in a sky you can't see a hundred feet in.'

Casting an evil glare at the nature surrounding them, Erina got back to helping Josh haul debris out of the way. The shuttle might never be able to fly again, and the airlock led only to a wall of compacted rock and dirt[2], but the bay doors at the stern worked — after a fashion — and she sure wasn't going to sleep out here, in the open.

Sure, they weren't seeing anything that looked remotely dangerous (unless

---

[2] Technically it was a "floor" of rock and dirt, the portside door now leading distinctly downwards.

the numerous rabbits that had started appearing grew fangs after dark). But she'd rather have several inches of plastasteele between her and this unknown world until she was sure it wasn't going to come after her. And even then— No, she'd bet this place wasn't anywhere near as empty as it looked like at the moment.

Having a huge fireball descend on you and explode sent most creatures running. Humans were the only ones she knew of that, right after, would begin rushing back to *find out* what had happened, in case it was dangerous, or, possibly, amusing. Oh, and dragons. Dragons did that too. Of course, *they* were well armoured to deal with things if anything large and tentacley began to emerge.

Also, she didn't want to get wet. This place, it was an overabundance of green — the colour — in a million shades she had no names for, practically assaulted your eyes from every direction but up, and even she knew that, to get that, you also had to have a fair bit of water. Since it didn't look like there were any rivers nearby that moisture had to come from above.

Working with the fervour of the royally pissed off, Erina pushed and pulled and hacked at any bit of debris that was foolish enough to put up a fight. She didn't like having her life dictated to her by some uppity bit of nature and she certainly wasn't going to take snark from some machine.

If she wanted water to rain on her, she'd get in the shower — which had the added bonus of being hot. Too bad there wasn't one of those around, she thought as another piece of metal clanged its way through the wide open doors to land in a nearby pile.

The rest of the day was taken up by clearing out the insides of the shuttlecraft — ensuring them a safe place to sleep.

Unfortunately, it wasn't only broken bits of technology that needed attending to. Amongst the general rubble, there were bits and pieces of the other passengers.

'Yuck,' Erina scrunched up her face as something blue and gooey dropped on her head. The smell was pungent to say the least. It might make for good circuitry, but only when inside the tubes and packs that contained it. On contact with air it took on a distinct, stomach-turning, aroma.

'Biosealant. Gross.'

Scraping it off with a disgusted look, she turned to ask Josh to help her only to realize he was no longer there. He was outside, puking his guts out.

Not his literal guts, thankfully (that would have been really gross), even though it sure sounded like it. The noise turned her own stomach. She could feel the bile rising in her throat.

Oh no you don't, she snapped at her insides, careful to keep her mouth closed, in case opening it gave her twisting gut ideas.

Thankfully, for both their sakes, apart from that one, the remaining passengers didn't require a stomach of iron to remove, and, eventually, they managed to drag them all out onto the grass.

The passengers, as well as the two other crew members from the *Random Star,* they buried nearby. After first stripping them of anything useful, that was. Something that earned Erina dark looks from Josh.

'What? *They're* not going to need them!' she snapped at him. 'Who knows, we might be grateful for a change of clothes later.'

The junior crewman clearly wasn't impressed, though he did, reluctantly, help her. Erina almost wished he hadn't bothered, as he kept hesitating and it ended up taking twice as long as it should have.

'Aren't you gonna say a few words over them, Cognitor?' Josh asked later as they patted down the last bits of dirt at the burial site.

'Why? Think it'd help them?' Erina enquired, raising an eyebrow over her shoulder.

'It'd help *me*,' Josh mumbled under his breath as they treaded back towards the downed shuttle, taking care that his companion didn't hear.

'The *Random Star's* gonna come looking for us,' he insisted later, as, after a lot of lifting and cleaning, they prepared to dig into the evening's meal of stale rations. 'They'll find us for sure. You could have just piled some rocks on them. That's what you do, at times like this.'

'Really?'

'Mhm.'

'Good luck finding that many stones hiding in the grass,' Erina scoffed. 'And if anyone was going to come rescue us *quickly*, they should have been here already.'

'They'll come,' Josh insisted.

He always sounded terribly optimistic about that, Erina decided later. If the circumstances had been different, he might even have had a point. The *Random Star*, while not a large vessel, was much better equipped in terms of sensors than any shuttle. Even if the ship was out of range from their end, the opposite need not apply.

Logic suggested that once the shuttle hadn't checked in, the bigger ship would come looking for them.

A wry smile tugged at a corner of her lips as she thought about that. Electricity didn't seem to work here. Nothing that *used* electric currents worked here. Heck, the whole bloody place hadn't shown up on *any* of their sensors. Why should it show up on anyone else's?

If it had, then how come no one had ever heard about it before? It wasn't like it was the type of valley that was small and easy to disguise. So, if no one had ever known it was there, what in that suggested that any other signals, theirs included, would escape to be heard?

Casticia might be sparsely populated, as most newly settled planets were, but she doubted anyone would be able to hide a place like this in a *normal* manner.[3]

No, they were going to be stuck here for some time. And if they wanted to leave, they were going to have to find the way themselves. The big question wasn't who (that one was obvious) but how.

She still hadn't worked out that bit — yet.

With those thoughts tumbling over and over, like rambunctious eels released into the wild, Erina drifted off into a restless sleep.

---

[3] Crashed into by colonists going somewhere else entirely was more like it. Casticia wasn't a normal type of planet. But then *the Orion* hadn't been your normal type of colony-ship…

CHAPTER THREE

'What was that?' Erina jerked back involuntarily.

She'd been peeking out of one of the two rear portholes, trying to see in the near pitch blackness beyond, when something had looked back.

'What was what?' Josh asked, raising his eyes from the mechanical trinket in his lap. He'd been trying to put it back together for three nights. So far, Erina had no idea what it was supposed to do, if anything.

'I saw … something. There, in the porthole,' Erina pointed. 'It was *looking* at us. At me.'

Josh examined the ink black glass from where he sat. 'It's not there now.'

It didn't take much to come to that conclusion, Erina thought. The porthole, transparent that it might be on a normal day, was sitting there like a dollop of solidified darkness, flat and, she noticed, slightly damp.

Had something been breathing on it? On the outside.

'Obviously it's not there now,' she intoned. 'Or you'd see it.'

Aside from the slightly unnerving experience of suddenly being stared into, she had a feeling he didn't believe her. When you gazed into the abyss, it might well gaze back — but it wasn't supposed to do it with a big, ruddy eyeball.

Josh, in turn, watched her cautiously as she placed a hand on the glass. Her nose scrunched up against the plate, Erina tried to pierce the darkness beyond. Again, there was nothing.

But the night was always unwilling to give up its secrets, she knew. It twisted your consciousness and turned your vision around again and again until you had no idea what you'd actually seen. A rose petal could turn into a monster, a nightmare into a wheel. Shadows always played tricks on you.

But something had been there. And she knew an eye when she saw one. A big, red orb just hovering in ink, glowing like a Deadman's Lantern.

She mentally kicked herself. It wasn't like her to jump at shadows … or eyes. Her right hand clenched, as if grasping an imaginary weapon. It might calm her beating heart, but it wouldn't do much good if whatever was out there came knocking.

To make extra certain, in case it did, Erina double-checked the lock on the bay doors. Good, that was secure.

Now, if only the viewscreen wasn't clear and large enough to accommodate an entire creature; even a large one might fit, especially if they leapt in with their legs tucked close to their body.

She shuddered.

Stop being such an idiot, Erina scolded herself. Those windows can withstand the impact of a small asteroid. It's not going to be shattered by a flesh-and-blood predator looking for an easy meal hiding in their burrow.

Not that, that wasn't what she felt like, cooped up in here.

'If that wasn't an eye, then I'm a one-legged hopmonkey,' she muttered under her breath as she, eventually, settled down for the night.

In the other makeshift bunk on the floor, Josh was already snoring. It took several more hours until Erina herself finally fell asleep.

It was the morning light that proved her right. Though Josh was the first awake — as usual — his foray into the fresh air came to an abrupt stop; the bucket slipping from his hands, clanging against the side of the hull.

Eyes wide, the young crewman retreated inside the shuttle at speed. Stumbling over a pile of carefully stacked thingies, he ended up tumbling into the wall.

A small yelp escaped him as he nearly speared himself somewhere painfully. Jerking back, he knocked into some loose circuit boards, sending the whole set tumbling and clanging.

'What the blasters is all that noise?' Erina yelled groggily.

'Oh, good! Cognitor. You're awake!' Josh's audible sigh of relief was almost as loud as his earlier yelp had been.

'Like anyone could sleep with the racket you're making,' Erina muttered.

She yawned wildly, drowsily scanning the immediate surroundings for any threat. 'What's going on? An alien invasion?'

'I saw 'em! Out there. I saw. Come. Come quick.' Josh hopped from foot to foot.

'Saw what?' Erina jolted awake as if slapped. She had no desire to get eaten in her sleep. 'Is it still here? Where? What?'

'No. No. Outside. Come. I'll show yah!'

Realizing there wasn't any immediate danger, Erina resisted the urge to roll over and go back to sleep. After another heavy yawn, she reluctantly forced herself up and into the light.

The ground beneath where the porthole was, there the earth was all churned up — and not from the crash either. Even she could see that. It was fresh too — well, compared to their arrival. So something *had* been sneaking around in the dark.

'Those are tracks,' she said. The moment the words escaped her lips, she wanted to knock herself over the head with a cast-iron pan. Thanks for pointing out the obvious, dumb brain.

Snorting at her own morning idiocy, she turned her head this way, then that. Staring at the footprints didn't bring as much insight as a growing sense of dread.

'Could be hooves,' Josh suggested after staring at the tracks for a while. He kept glancing over his shoulder. 'Do hooves have claws?'

Erina shrugged. 'I'll be darned if I know. It's got four feet — I think — and it's bigger than we are. Either that, or there were a whole bunch of them here last night. Look at how many imprints there are.'

She scanned their surroundings but the early morning haze made it difficult to make out anything specific. The distant treeline was a faint, fuzzy brown with a touch of greenish vagueness. If she hadn't known there were trees there, she probably wouldn't have guessed it.

It would have lent a certain amount of serenity to the day, turning everything into soft pastels, if her mind hadn't been preoccupied with what was staring up at them from the ground.

Still, things could be worse…

'At least it's not eyeballs[4],' Erina said.

'Hugh, what?'

'Forget it. I don't know about you, but I don't think I care for sharing this place with whatever that is,' Erina pointed to the ground. 'Things with claws can be a bit picky about their neighbours.'

'Are you sure those are claws?'

'No. But they don't look like ordinary hooves to me either. Do you want to find out for sure? You can stay outside tonight and ask it, why don't you?'

Josh withdrew a bit. He was already having trouble telling plain orders from sheer sarcasm. He'd always wondered what it was like, working with the Cognitor. Ever since Erina had joined the crew it had turned from a non-job into something sounding glamorous, adventurous, and other things ending in -ous. Despite that, most people never volunteered for those missions. Now he was beginning to understand why.

Odd, he thought. The Captain never had any trouble. Neither did the Medical Officer for some reason.

'Well, we'll never get anything done standing around staring at this all day,' Erina slapped her hands down. 'I'm sick of being cooped up in that tiny space. Maybe it's time we got a good look at this place. Let's go exploring, shall we?'

She could have sworn Josh turned a shade paler at that, but he didn't say anything.

Everyone always told you that, if anything happened, you shouldn't stray far from the crash site. That the first place anyone would come looking, would be said site.

That's certainly what the manual said too.

Ah, what did some pages on her diom know, Erina made a "pfft" noise. There wasn't anything in the manual for being lost in a world with no name, no hope of rescue and, if they were *really* unlucky, no escape.

'But—' Josh protested.

'Do you really *want* to eat nothing but nutrilicious bars for the rest of your

---

[4] Big glowy eyeballs generally spelt trouble. Floating ones were bad enough, but the ones still in their own sockets often came with teeth attached. Big, sharp, teeth. Mouths were optional.

days?'

'NO!'

'Didn't think so,' Erina made a half-amused sound. 'There's bound to be other things to eat around here. We've already seen rabbits. Now, let's see if we can catch one.'

She began stuffing things into her makeshift satchel with a, 'See, I told you all that extra material would come in handy.'

Josh raised an eyebrow at her as she, automatically, packed her blaster — despite the fact that it didn't work.

Several hours later, Erina was grateful for her rach-hide boots. They were supple, fitting like a glove. Also, they didn't chafe. No. She didn't envy Josh who trudged across the plain in his space boots. They might be great for wandering around a nice, even-levelled spaceship and taking trips into the big, black, vacuum without having to change your footwear, but, for slightly muddy grasslands, not so much.

'There's got to be more to this place than grass and rabbits,' Erina complained, throwing herself on the ground with a grunt. 'I swear we've walked for miles and that's *all* we've seen.'

'They do kind of go together. Grass and rabbits I mean. And they're not exactly rabbits.'

'Okay, they're *weird* rabbits. Small. Furry. Runs when they see you. Dig,' here she shook her foot. The one that had stepped into a burrow. It was still a bit sore. 'The fact that they're blue doesn't stop them from being rabbits.'

'Not all of them are.'

'True. I'm surprised they're here at all though. I mean, even a near-sighted eagle should have no trouble picking up on these guys. It's not like they're heavy on the camouflage.'

'Maybe it's something they eat?' Josh suggested.

'Could be. A lot of poisonous things have been painted neon. So the rabbits are immune, but whatever eats rabbits isn't, so it doesn't. That makes sense.'

Erina took a long drink from the travelling flask and leaned back. Watching the sky, it had that summer blueness to it that you got up north — it even had the soft, cotton clouds — but, judging from the nature around them, it wasn't summer. Spring was more likely. It even smelled like it. Slightly warm grass. Flowers just beginning to bud. A crispness to the air when you breathed. No, spring made sense.

'Imagine if we'd crashed here in the middle of winter?'

'I don't think I would have liked that,' Josh shuddered.

'Me neither,' Erina agreed. 'Look at this place. Maybe we picked the wrong direction to walk in. You can still see the wreck, look.' She pointed at a small speck in the distance. 'We should have gone into the woods.'

'The ground seems to go up a bit ahead,' Josh said, squinting. 'Maybe we could get a better view from there?'

'What are we waiting for then? Old age? Let's go.'

Climbing onto the outcropping Josh had spotted earlier proved easier said than done.

Erina was willing to swear that the outcropping kept moving since, by the time they actually reached it, her throbbing thighs forced her to sit down in its shadow and rest. It also turned out to be a lot steeper than it had looked from a distance. Less craggy, more sheer.

'What d'you think you are? Bloody Cliffs of Doom or something?' Erina snarled up at it.

In her mind, rock should be solid and dependable. This stuff was as brittle as a skittle in a food processor. As such, it took a fair amount of not very ladylike language to finally propel her to the top.

When she eventually threw the satchel over the summit and heaved herself after it, Josh was already there and had even brought out some of the sparse flimsies, the backsides of which they'd been using to make a map.

He was holding it up against the suns, which had begun their descent, to check the directions. So much for getting here before noon, Erina sighed. She shaded her eyes. Most of the suns were barely visible and then only if you squinted really hard and knew they were there. Natural sunlight should have cooked the world to a charcoaled crisp. Instead it was bathed in a warm, pleasant, yellow.

'Well, suppose if I needed confirmation there's lots of trees here, I came to the right place.' Erina muttered mutinously as she tried to catch her breath from the ascent. 'We go up. Suns go down. Makes perfect sense. Not.'

'We came from over there,' Josh jabbed a finger in the air.

Nodding, Erina couldn't argue with that. 'Doesn't look that far, does it?'

'No, it doesn't. And that's strange.'

'Felt like it, though,' Erina said. She rubbed at her arms. She wasn't used to climbing rocks. Most of her work took her to more civilized parts.

Also, when climbing buildings, bringing the right tools made the job a whole lot easier. So did making sure you could just walk through the main door with no one being the wiser.

It turned out that they weren't all that far from the crash site after all, so everything between the outcropping and the ship was mostly grassy plains with the occasional cluster of leafy, green trees swaying gently in the breeze.

Odd that they hadn't passed any of those when walking here, she thought. Maybe they were growing in depressions or something. That'd explain not seeing them. She couldn't think of anything else that would. It wasn't like you just walked past a tree out in the middle of nothing and didn't notice.

As Josh said: odd.

Turning around, in the opposite direction, that seemingly endless grass-land wasn't endless at all. There was a touch of darkness to the blue at the horizon that suggested there might be more than another mountain range there. And before that, there was another colour. It was much, much closer. Even at this distance, there was a hint of green. Dark green.

'Great. More bloody trees.'

They were too far away to make out what sort, but, in the remaining two directions, what Erina kept thinking of as "normal" trees, were growing denser and denser and, from the look of things, climbing the foothills behind them. At those sides, the treeline wasn't actually anywhere near as far from the crash site as she would have thought.

The endless plains had become a wide stretch of hills and grass bordered by more vertically inclined neighbours.

'From below, all I could see was tree trunks. From up here, all I can see are tree crowns. Great improvement, eyes.'

There were slim ones. Thick ones. Brown, grey, black, even green ones (though Erina was willing to bet that was moss) clambering all over each other to steal sunlight from the trees next door.

'Guess it was too much to ask for a radio mast or two,' Erina sighed. It would have been nice if they hadn't been the first ones shipwrecked here.

'Sign on, they said. See the stars, they said. Widen your horizons. Bah. ALL I've GOT now are horizons — wouldn't hurt if they threw in a little civilization. You know, just to brighten things up?'

Josh was pointedly ignoring her mutterings. As long as it was the trees she was growling at and not him, he was happy.

Erina kicked a bit of loose gravel and watched it bounce its way down the outcropping in increasingly numerous pieces before burying itself in one of the sparse tufts of grass that grew in the nooks and crannies.

Turning her attention back to what she should be doing, Erina scanned the horizon for any useful clues to where they were. Josh, in the meantime, was busy mapping out distances. Since there were no survey maps of this strange place, any map at all was better than none, even if it was a bit hard to make out what he was drawing.

'Well, hello, hello, what do we have here?'

Erina perked up at the sight she'd just caught. It wasn't exactly a space-port, but amongst the hazy paleness there was a sparkle of blue. A twinkle of reflections in the sunlight.

It was barely visible, only a couple of snatches of imagery really. But, if they were closer, it was easy to imagine that it'd stretch out. A small lake then. Maybe even a river.

'Water,' Erina said. 'Some good news at last. 'course, we still need to actually find the blasted thing.'

First, they'd better return to the shuttle. Finding water was indeed great — more than great even. Their supply wasn't exactly running low, but Erina figured that it was better to diversify their assets rather than wait for them to run out and then scramble around madly trying to replace them. But just finding it didn't mean diddly squat if they couldn't bring it back.

'Man might be able to live off dehydrated food cubes alone, but compressed hyperdrops sure do taste like yesterday's old socks, before *and* after decompressing,' Erina grimaced at the thought.

Like so many others, she much preferred the second. It was hard convincing herself, and even more so, her stomach, that she had, in fact, had more than enough liquids just placing a drop or two on her tongue.

'Hmm, what?' Josh looked up from what he was doing.

'Never mind. Guess I shouldn't complain too much,' Erina mumbled to herself as they started their way back. 'They could have forgotten to store *any* emergency supplies on board.'

Maybe it was the extra bounce in their step from having found (hopefully) one of the essentials of life, but the return journey was much quicker than expected. Maybe it was just that they were heading *home* — a place somewhere out of the wind and with drinks to warm them.

There was, however, *one* slight detour.

It was as they were walking past a clump of what looked like cherries in full bloom (though Josh insisted that they were some sort of crab-apple trees, all Erina saw was a grove full of pink) that her companion made an excited squeal and dove in under the branches.

'Look,' he showed off his find, grinning. 'Mushrooms!'

'I can see that.'

Erina recoiled slightly as her companion enthusiastically picked several of those that grew on the largest trunk.

'Are you *absolutely* sure these are safe to eat?' she asked as Josh set about preparing them later, prodding the offending bits of vegetation with a hesitant finger.

'Yeah, I'm sure.'

'It feels kinda spongy to the touch,' she said, not looking convinced. 'I mean, we need protein, but *mushrooms*?'

'My ma used to cook these up a treat,' Josh assured her.

'See, they even have little white spots.'

'I'll have them done in a jiffy. Don't you worry, Cognitor.'

That night, the two castaways were left partially curled up. Occasionally there'd be a moan but even that took too much energy. They felt light and heavy at the same time. Their legs, when they moved at all, were sluggish, as were their arms. Most of the time they felt too weak to even lament their situation. Lobes swelled. Veins throbbed. And stomachs groaned and gurgled unhappily, turning their intestines into a route of pain.

The profuse sweating broke around midnight. The shivers lasted all the way into the morning and beyond. So did the misty film that had descended over their irises, leaving them stumbling around, waving their hands about, long after being able to actually stand again.

CHAPTER FOUR

A few days later and Erina welcomed the hike through the forest. It had taken longer than usual to get to the stream she'd found, but she put that down to still not feeling great.

'Next time I appoint someone to the protein acquisition committee, I'm damn well forbidding them to go near anything that looks even remotely like a mushroom,' Erina grumbled.

She swung the sharp blade they used when preparing food (and other things) with a vengeance, hacking the nutrilicious bar into tiny, tiny pieces, then tipped them into a metallic can and whisked them around.

Taking a drought of the resulting drink, the *yuck* sensation started in her feet, working its way up, until it reached her hairline and she shuddered.

'Glah,' she gagged. 'Gross.'

Turned out nutrilicious bars didn't taste at all better when dissolved.

She forced down the last bits, then took another mouthful of clean water from the canteen to rinse the taste out. It made her teeth chatter.

'Well, I found the stream at least,' Erina picked herself up and slung the second set of makeshift canteens over her shoulder with an, 'oomph.'

'Wish I'd known it was liquid ice before I stepped into it. Brrr. Must flow down from the mountains. Wouldn't have thought that it'd stay cool for that long though.'

Having left Josh to tend to the camp, so far this whole exploration malarkey had been rather dull, Erina thought. The most exciting thing to have happened was her startling a tiny herd of horses that had come to the stream to drink.

They must have thought she'd been something else, because they took flight the moment she stumbled through the rustling bushes. For a few milling moments, the air filled with neighs and whinnies and the clapping of hooves on the stony bank. Then they disappeared into the woods.

It was a while after the dust settled that she'd made herself comfortable on a nice, sunny, boulder. Close by, the bubbling stream splashed merrily across the stony ground. It moved ever downwards, as if the whole stream was just one, gentle waterfall — albeit a very shallow one with plenty of round stones peeking over the clear surface.

A little too wary to actually snooze out here, Erina nonetheless enjoyed letting some of the tension slip from her shoulders. The scent of fresh water, cool stones warming in the sun, and the brisk promise of summer arising from the leaves and bark in every breath was everything being cooped up in a spaceship wasn't. For a while, it wasn't interrupted by anything other than the chirping of birds and the calling of crickets.

Quiet, hesitant hoofbeats clip-clopped closer and closer. Erina's eyes — which had been enjoying the snooze — shot upwards at speed. Her ears tried to triangulate. A fist tightened around her heart. The blood to her fingers increased. Her right hand ever so slowly edged towards something sharp and pointy next to her.

Gradually turning her head, hoping to catch a glimpse of whatever had arrived — preferably without it seeing her — she heard several snorts from down by the stream.

They made her twitch but, on closer inspection, it was just one lone horse coming back to drink.

'What in the world are you doing?' Erina watched as the horse paced back and forth on the bank several times before entering the water. It looked like it really, really wanted a nice refreshing drink but was afraid the water was going to bite it. Once in, it kept shifting its legs fretfully — splashing water everywhere.

'So, where's the rest of you? Don't you guys usually live in herds? For you *are* a horse, aren't you? Even if you do look like an escapee from a harlequin convention.'

Rolling, slowly, over on her stomach, Erina was content for a time to just watch. She was still hidden, if getting somewhat cold, when the herd returned — apparently having decided that there wasn't anything that was going to eat them here after all — and the strangely coloured horse was driven off with squeals and feints and kicks.

'Not part of the team, eh? Well, I can relate to that.'

Erina quietly slipped off the rock, out of sight of the herd. She didn't want to scare them off twice in a row. Gathering up her gear, she began making her way back to camp.

Several hours later, the cognitor beat a heavy branch out of her way. Much of the undergrowth was full of shrubs that clung to your legs if you tried to walk through them, so Erina tried to stick to where the moss carpeted the ground.

While the ground was uneven, it was quite light and airy here, so there wasn't much moss. Instead, she had to push aside ferns or just force the shrubs into submission.

'I don't remember all this stuff from walking out here,' Erina muttered darkly. One of the beaten branches smacked her right back. 'Ouch! Ruddy tree.'

Erina slapped the offending trunk hard. While gnarly, the bark bore no trace of being other than natural. She shook her head.

'I left markers, I'm sure of it. Or I'd never find my way back.'

Turned out that even *with* the markers she'd gotten a bit turned around. While she was heading in the right direction, her current path was at a lower level than the one that originally brought her to the stream. This one was taking her through a shallow depression in the forest.

Almost impossible to spot from above, down here, the two paths might be in the same forest, leafy brothers even; but they were similar, not the same. The murky smell was damper. Stuffier. More oppressing.

With all the trees in the way, she hadn't realized she was going the wrong way … until now.

'Wait. What was that?' Erina stomped her feet on the green sponge — eh, no, moss — that had invaded what served as ground around here.

'That's odd,' she muttered. 'Could have sworn something echoed just now. Wonderful, now I'm hearing things too. My life really is complete.'

A few steps later, and the sound rang out again. Only, it wasn't exactly ringing.

It seemed to be coming up through her boots. She paused experimentally, in case it was caused by her own movements. No. There it was again. Closer this time.

Kneeling down, she patted the velvet carpet. 'Nope, that's moss alright. So…' Glancing around, the ground was clearly elevated and uneven, with sharp angular shapes. Shrugging, she knelt down and started pulling at it.

'I'm not losing out to some stupid plant,' Erina snarled five minutes later after she'd pulled out her knife. Scraping away the living cover, the blade suddenly rang out against stone.

'Well, that's one less mystery then. Just normal bedrock. Thought it might have been building blocks or something. Wonder if it's stone all the way down?' She put her ear to the ground. 'Nope, still hear it. Just fainter now. Stones don't speak, do they? It'd explain a lot, if they did. No?'

The carpet was silent on the matter, though somewhere she could hear the chirping of insects.

'Wonder if this thing's hollow?' Erina stamped her heel down hard a couple of times. It sounded pretty solid to her. That didn't stop the reverberant vibrations from echoing forth from below. For several minutes, they grew steadily, then, as mysteriously as they had appeared, they faded away.

'If I didn't know better, I'd swear something just passed straight underneath me. No?' Erina shook her head. 'That's crazy. The ground's not hollow. No one's built a freight tunnel here … have they?'

Brushing the dirt off her hands, she replaced the knife in its sheath and, giving the whole thing a few more kicks for good measure, headed back towards where she should have been going in the first place.

Growing tired and annoyed[5], Erina stomped through the forest sending squirrels dashing away on leafy branches and things scurrying into their hidey-holes. Not that she noticed. In fact, it took a while before she realized

---

[5] Not a good combination at the best of times, the world was lucky Erina couldn't just stomp it all out of existence.

that the woods around her were going quiet she was so busy thinking about other things.

Now, Erina threw an eye over her shoulder. 'Come out, come out, wherever you are,' the trees seemed to rustle.

The woods were sparse here, barely more than collections of young stems and a bit of bracken. You could even see the plains beyond now — if you looked really carefully. The suns were still high in the sky, scattering light through the myriad of branches over her head. It should have been just another peaceful stroll.

But something had changed. The forest felt a lot darker. Shadows seemed to come alive. Were they closing in on her? The downy hair on her arms rose. Whether it was from electricity in the air or worry was hard to say.

'Don't be silly,' Erina scolded herself. But she did so in hushed tones. 'Trees don't speak. You're not going to go crazy on top of everything else, d'you hear? But there's *something* there, I'm sure of it.'

Speaking barely above a whisper, her eyes narrowed. She sniffed several times. There didn't seem to be any strange scents, just the normal, musty woodland smells.

Despite the lack of a threat appearing, Erina wished she had a stout oak staff — even a bent and gnarly one would do — or, better yet, something with a serious edge to it. Something a whole lot bigger than the knife quietly pulled from its sheath. Something that would have felt comforting as she gripped its hilt.

'Blast that blaster,' Erina growled. Despite trying to conserve the charge it had run out ridiculously soon after the crash. Straight away even.

It wasn't going to help now. The best she could hope for was to knock someone over the head with it — and she hadn't brought it today to begin with.

Eyes swivelled, trying to see everything around her, above and below. Wait. Was that a shadow?

All at once, her body tensed.

There was movement. Someone, or something, drifted in and out of view. Always silently. Always just beyond where she could see clearly. Light and shadow in one.

So something WAS out there, Erina thought. Something big.

Erina did the only sensible thing she could think of. She hightailed it out of there.

Whatever it was didn't seem to follow her.

Since Erina never told her companion about what she'd seen in the woods, not being sure of it herself, he should have remained blissfully unaware of it. But words are only one type of communication.

That he soon cottoned on to that something wasn't quite right, might well have had something to do with how their collection of knick-knacks became strewn all over the site; some of it thrown aside quite forcefully.

Erina wasn't even sure it was the same creature. Or if what she'd seen had been a creature at all. It could have been a sort of extra concentrated luminescent ghost.

On the other hand, this latest intruder at least appeared to be flesh and blood.

'What'cha looking for, Cognitor? I could help?' Josh asked.

'Hmm, no, not this either.'

Josh dodged the broken tool as it came flying. All the carefully constructed assemblies were a mess. He sighed.

'Cognitor?'

'What? Oh, hey. Didn't see you there. Can I help you with something?'

'What's going on?'

'This? Oh. I just fancied a little something. Sharp and to the point, if you know what I mean,' Erina inspected another piece then tossed that aside too. 'Who knows what might be lurking around here when we're not looking?'

'Should I get something too?'

'You know. That might not be a bad idea.' Erina stopped in the middle of the sentence to frown. 'Hey, do you even know how to use a weapon?'

'Sure thing, Cognitor,' Josh dropped to one knee, mimicking the stance of a shooter. 'I'm fully checked out on blasters. Just point and shoot really.' He went, 'Pfft! Pfft!' grinning wildly.

Erina rolled her eyes. 'This isn't some wild wastes entertainment show, you know. With risk of repeating myself. Have you. Ever. Shot. At. Anything. Outside. Practice?'

'Sure have. On stun,' her companion added a bit sheepishly after a moment's hesitation.

'Wonderful. You'll be a great help if the blasters ever decide to work again.'

'Oops. Forgot 'bout that.'

'I noticed. Me, I'm going with something a little more old-fashioned,' Erina hefted one of the peculiarly shaped durasteel pieces she'd set aside. It was longer than her arm, curving gently.

'Don't get me wrong. I'd be a lot happier hitting them from afar before they even know I'm there, but beggars can't be choosers … or so I've heard.'

She would indeed have been happier with something even longer but trying to sharpen bits of durasteel or plastasteele had proven, if not futile, so certainly frustratingly slow. They were, after all, made to withstand the rigours of space travel. Durability was practically their middle names. "Turn into amazing blades that cuts through anything in five minutes," was not.

The bits and pieces that *were* sharp, were so courtesy of the crash. There was nothing like hitting itself at high speed that got even the strongest material into a contest of what would break first. Somehow, Erina didn't think two humans would be able to exert quite the same force — though not from lack of trying.

Several days later, taking a few swings with the result of their efforts, Erina twirled over the grass, her steps lighter than Josh had ever seen them. It was like watching a stumbling elephant turn into a leaping antelope before your very eyes.

'Somehow, I just can't see myself chasing down rabbits or deer with this thing,' she smiled, a dark twinkle in her eyes. 'It does have a nice feel though. I'll take it. Just need to wrap the handle. It keeps slipping out of my grip.'

'Does that mean we can have a break now?' Josh asked. He slid down the hull. They'd spent hours and hours, no days, gathering together a small collection that could be used as weapons.

He wondered how effective they would be against what might live here.

'Have you seen anything lately?' Erina asked while they were collecting wood for the fire one day.

When Josh shook his head, Erina bit her lip. Just because they hadn't seen anything, that didn't mean they weren't there.

They both knew they weren't talking about their midnight visitor – as mysterious as that one continued to be.

'There's an old saying; *where there's smoke, there's fire*,' Erina mused. 'Or, in this case, where there's bones, there's a body.'

'*Was* a body.'

Some of them had been pretty big bones at that. The remains of ribcages, bleached by the sun, half buried in the turf. It was too bad they couldn't tell how old they were. Or *what* they were. There weren't any dragons here, were there?

If any of those had been lost, she was sure they'd have heard about it. Dragons were, after all, still a rarity on her world. If caught by this infernal valley and lived out their days without being able to return to the world from whence they'd come, they'd succumb to old age the same as any other.

But since no dragon was over their thirties, she somehow doubted they belonged to anyone she knew.

'Too bad, we could have done with the help.' Erina shrugged. 'Nothing like a big, bad dragon on your side to send smaller predators running. And in this place, I bet *everything* is smaller than a dragon.'

'You sure, Cognitor? I mean, they don't really fit under all those trees.'

'True that,' Erina admitted. 'And it's not like they can breathe fire, but still…'

And then there was that mysterious visitor that kept invading their camp at night. Putting up torches hadn't fazed them for long, not once they'd learnt that they didn't last all night — turning into brittle embers long before dawn.

Then there were other little things they found when out exploring. Like shed horns easily as large, or larger, than she was, reclaimed by the mossy ground on which they'd fallen. Or tufts of tails, caught amongst branches high above them.

'I'm telling you, Josh,' she said. 'They're out there. Prey this large, you can bet your sorry ass that there's gonna be predators that big too.'

'Hope not,' Josh muttered.

'You hear them last night? Something moving? Snuffling and whuffing to itself. Sounded like there were more than one. Either that or it had more than one head.'

Erina had seen a lot. The latter wasn't completely impossible.

'So, does that mean these are the native species of the planet?' Erina mused later that night while chewing unenthusiastically on a food cube.

They still hadn't had much luck with securing a local food source. Game was harder to trap in the real world than entertainment made it out to be. Birds just flew away. What berries and fruit there were, were far from ripe in spring. And it was the wrong time of the year entirely for most nuts they could actually recognize.

'The early colonists[6], once they'd begun to survey the planet, they didn't find much in the way of larger animals, did they?'

'Don't think so.'

'No. A bit short on the large, big and scaly really. Even in the oceans. These things, it's like they're in a whole different league.'

If anything, they reminded her of some of the hybrids. Bred by those early colonists to adapt to the new world, and its dangers; big and small, many of the results had been unique (and not always very safe to be around) but a few had successfully carved out a niche in the changing ecosystem.

As such, the world was growing ever more complex each day, and not just because of their creations. It seemed they constantly found new species too, whole new sections of whatever breathed life into this world. Some of those, no one seemed to be able to explain where they'd come from either. They didn't appear quite out of the blue, but once some random explorer or surveyor stumbled upon them in a secluded location far from everything, they quickly spread, as if they'd just waited for a chance.

---

[6] Well, crash landed, shipwrecked and very, very lost colonists anyway, but colonists all the same.

'Could there be more places like this?' Erina wondered. 'I mean, they could come from places like this and we'd never know. No one's ever seen or heard of them before. No one's ever seen or heard of this place either — or if they have, they haven't lived to tell about it.

'Could places like these really hide from *all* our sensors?' Josh wondered.

'Why not?' Erina shrugged. 'This place did.'

Over the coming days and weeks, they became more and more familiar with their immediate surroundings. The woods no longer spooked them as often and getting lost wasn't as much of a concern — unless they strayed too far.

Almost every day, Erina would climb to the top of the wreckage to check on what was happening nearby.

The sounds, the trilling of birds, or the scampering away of tiny shapes into the undergrowth, no longer put them on edge. Now they'd only start to really worry when the ambient noise of the forest, the glades, disappeared.

And it did, every now and then. It wasn't every day or every night, but it happened regularly. Since nothing more exciting happened during those times, no losses of arms or legs in a flurry of red, that too became familiar and, just a little bit boring.

Occasionally, Erina would catch the sight of something large and blueish. Then she'd blink, and it'd be gone.

Her trips to the nearest source of water they knew of became more frequent as well. Now that they'd found it, it made sense to keep the hyperdrops for emergencies only, though she had to admit she didn't particularly care for lugging heavy makeshift canteens, bottles, and anything else that could easily transport liquids around — especially not through a forest with no trails. Albeit, by now, one was slowly forming.

'Oh, look. My very own road … in ten years or so,' she'd quip whenever she saw it and was in the mood.

Every day, she grew more accustomed to the sights. Her footing grew safer; her ears now listening for subtle changes in the background rather than the hum of an engine, the swooshing of a door, or the beeping of some electronic device.

Sometimes, she'd see herds in the distance. Animals she had no name for. Horses galloping across the plains, manes streaming in the wind.

In the forests, there were boars (who didn't make much noise until you stumbled over them, after which they made a great deal of it); various forms of deer; and a multitude of more solitary creatures. Not to mention birds, squirrels and bugs.

To be honest, she could have done without the bugs.

Also, thanks to her frequent trips to the stream, the jester-like horse no longer startled and ran for it the moment he saw her.

You didn't see the rest of the forest herd often, but she could usually rely on him being there, somewhere. You wouldn't have thought that something — someone — with colours so striking — red as blood, white as snow, black as obsidian — could hide amongst all the green and browns, but he did.

While never venturing close enough to touch, the tri-coloured horse seemed to delight in sneaking up on her as she trained her sword skills; he'd snap playfully at some fluttering garment then dash away again as quick as could be.

'Well, you're sure light on your feet, I admit that,' Erina shook her head at her four-footed friend's antics as he pranced about on the banks of the stream. 'If I tried that, I'd break a leg or two.'

To Josh and Erina, it might have been safer not to, but it soon became clear that to get anything done, they needed to divide up the tasks of staying alive here between them.

This suited Erina fine. She wasn't about to give up her new-found sense of freedom. Having another human being underfoot wasn't her idea of restful — whether they were quiet, busy, or even asleep.

And so Josh was increasingly taking over the management of the camp. Keeping things shipshape and spending any time left over tinkering, appeared to keep him happy. Well, as happy as anyone could be when stranded far from home with no known way to return.

Normally, it was Erina who felt better after being allowed to bash things with a rock, but every time Josh would present her with his new creations, there would be this small, almost smug grin, on his face.

'Told ya spears would be easy to make,' he'd said only yesterday, holding out a slim lance-like rod with what appeared to be a hammered-out piece of scrap console strapped in on top.

'I'm not saying you're wrong,' Erina had said while twirling the piece with both hands. 'They're good spears. But I'd be happier with something I don't have to let go of to actually use.'

'It's not hard,' Josh had protested.

'Not for you. You actually hit what you aim at. Me, not so much. Maybe we should try making another sword or maybe even a scythe? Always thought scythes looked really cool.'

Josh had looked at her dubiously. He could try — he'd seemed to say — but she shouldn't expect any miracles. There weren't a lot of plastasteele pieces the right shape that also happened to be sharp. Finding bits for the spears had been relatively easy, but things like swords, even a makeshift one, required something far more elaborate.

So, deciding they could cover twice the area, twice the amount of tasks done and thereby, have twice the chance to succeed, Erina and Josh found themselves slowly drifting into different roles.

It didn't necessarily always happen without arguing.

'Where in this arrangement did it say I suddenly have to do ALL the food shopping?' Erina grumbled as she beat the nearest bushes with a branch, hoping to scare something up.

Admittedly, that *might* have something to do with that, after several bouts of indigestion and worse, she now eyed anything Josh brought back through distrustful slits and promptly refused to eat it, no matter how delicious it might look.

As a result, she'd gotten quite adept at catching rabbits, but that hardly felt sporting. It wasn't like they had much of a chance. Not once you learnt the trick anyway.

The deer and other animals she saw about in the woods, if she saw them at all, were always too far away to do anything about it or she didn't have the right tools with her. Erina didn't fancy trying to run down any of those on foot and projectile weapons weren't really her thing. Traps were more her style.

But she eyed everything suspiciously, practically expecting a surprise to emerge from the bushes and cause a ruckus. Most of the time, there was nothing there. But this was pretty much the default state for her, even when she *wasn't* marooned millions of miles from where she wanted to be, and she paid it little mind.

To be honest, it wasn't exactly like she "wanted" to scuttle back and forth among the planets of the solar system like a billiard ball with attitude. It was just that she hadn't found anything better to do … yet.

She had to keep reminding herself of that last bit every once in a while (and every few minutes during some assignments) to keep from finding another unknown looking more interesting.

If the universe had cared to ask her beforehand[7], the wilds would not have been her first choice to begin a new career; if you could call "surviving" a career. The prospects of promotions were, after all, slim.

'I couldn't have gotten stranded somewhere sensible? No-ooo. Like a place with restaurants and shops?'[8]

'Take away. Take away is good,' she licked her lips. 'Like that nice little place where we dock for maintenance. Old station. Brilliant food. Bit oily maybe.'

Gods, she could almost taste their fried dumplings on her tongue right now.

No. Bad idea. Erina shook herself. 'Stop thinking about past stuff and find something to bloody well cook. You can do that at least, can't you?'

Normally, their dioms would hold much of the information needed on flora and fauna. Certainly on the inner planets and if you didn't stray too far from any known settlements.

'It'd sure be handy right now to know what's perfectly safe to eat only after boiling it, turning three times around a spruce, and sacrificing a small goat,' Erina grumped and rolled her eyes.

---

[7] It never did.
[8] Not that she actually frequented either much. She just thought they lent a certain "je ne sais quoi" to the background. Also, the busy ones were good for losing people chasing you.

Wrapping the diom around her wrist, she glared at the, normally, so relia-
ble device. 'Two thousand fathoms down or floating in the vacuum of space,
and this thing is still your digital friend. But here? Nooo. You'd think they'd
design these for *all* eventualities. Hah!'

This place though, there were so many things that looked vaguely familiar
from a distance, only to prove to be something else entirely when scrutinized
up close.

'Let's face it, girl. If the dioms were working, you wouldn't be in this
pickle in the first place,' she muttered and pushed aside a particularly stubborn branch away from her eyes.

A welcoming whinny immediately made her day better.
'Good Morning,' Erina greeted the tri-coloured painted horse with a great
deal more enthusiasm than she'd usually spare for any of her colleagues, as
she dropped the improvised canisters on the rocky bank.

A small, curved set of equine ears flickered in her direction as she spoke,
but, otherwise, he seemed content to ignore her today. She knew that was just
a ruse.

'These stones are going to be the death of my feet,' she announced, referring to the rocky bed the water gurgled forth over. 'You have no idea how
lucky you are to have hooves.'

He snorted, blowing out air from his delicate nostrils and nibbled on a soft
looking set of plants Erina had no name for.

Make that "pretend" to ignore her, Erina thought. She'd learnt the hard
way that he was a curious creature at heart — albeit a cautious one.

This didn't extend to inanimate objects though, which was why she kept a
close hold of the containers. Last time, he'd waited until she was right in the
middle of the stream (it wasn't very deep, but it did spread out — as if to
compensate) before sneaking up and making off with one of them.

'You sure you're not some big dog in disguise?' she asked. 'A really, really big dog? Fetch? Know that one? Fetch? No?'

The horse looked at her, wondering what this peculiar two-legs was up to
this time.

CHAPTER FIVE

Erina was woken by an insistent pattering on the "roof" of the shuttle. Blinking groggily and looking out of the nearest viewport, it took a moment before she realized that it was streaked with water.

Ah, some part of her brain said — being more of an early bird than the rest of her — rain. That explained the pitter-patter. It wasn't millions of tiny feet. Just raindrops. Lots and lots of raindrops.

'Who cares?' Erina shrugged and turned over to try and get back to sleep — it was still way, way too early for waking up — when something nearby went, 'plink.'

Plink. Plink. Plink, went the droplets. Bouncing on the surface right next to her pillow, creating little miniature reversed explosions of wetness, they merrily went about destroying what little electronic circuitry might have remained.

Turning bleary eyes at the interior of the shuttle, Erina realized the reason why everything smelled so damp was because it *was* damp. The torrent outside had found a way inside.

'Oh joy, an indoor shower at last.' She glared at it. The rain wasn't intimidated.

Plink.

Since growling at the dropping water failed to stem the flow, she was forced out from underneath her cosy blankets. Her bare feet splashed onto the floor as she went to shake her companion awake at the other end of the shuttlecraft.

'Wait! What?' Josh woke with a start.

'That's what,' Erina stabbed her thumb at the ceiling where moisture trailed across the instruments, gathering, and then, with another, 'plink,' dropping straight down. 'Get up. And get some buckets or something or we're gonna float out of here.'

Throwing another murderous glare at the weather outside as light reluctantly brought in a new day. There wasn't a remote trace of a breeze down where they were. Above, the rain gushed forth from churning, brooding clouds and fell, absolutely, straight down creating small craters in the exposed earth and tiny fountain grenades on the rocks.

'Think it'll stop soon?'

'Doesn't look like.'

The two humans tried to mend the leaks as best they could, but the rain, while a new experience for them in this place, was obviously old and cunning. It found all the breaches, big, small, even microscopic, in the hull and promptly invaded them.

Eventually, they managed to plug the biggest ones. But, while the water was happily finding its way into the shuttle through all the cracks and whatnots created by the crash, it seemed loathed to leave the same way. In the end, they had to open the aft doors to allow it to run off.

'At least it's not windy,' Josh said, looking at the (now wet) things that they'd gathered in the shuttle. 'It could be worse.'

'Yeah, sure. Everything's just peachy now, isn't it?' Erina grumbled. Throwing her arms around her knees, she bundled up as best she could and watched the entryway with cold eyes and her shivering hands on her weapon.

Out, way beyond the confines of the metal shell of the downed craft from the stars, the rain continued to plummet from the sky. It filled waterholes that had been empty for years. Rivers and brooks overflowed, drowning nearby bushes or digging away under the roots of mighty willows until they fell, with a splash, into the increasingly fast-flowing currents.

Smaller mammals living close to the watercourses scurried towards higher ground where they could — climbing rocks, fallen trunks, or even whole trees — leading to a small war of chittering with the squirrels that normally called them home.

It drenched the nearby forests, turning lush, green lands into a haven for those whole liked mushy conditions or had a penchant for dams.

Everyone else wasn't nearly as pleased.

From the tallest mountains — where the rain wasn't rain, but large flakes of snow swirling around the top of Snowfell like a blizzard — to the foothills and lakelands below, it rained.

On the plains, the herds sought shelter where they could. Burrowers were forced out of their homes. The wall of wet drifted over the valley, shrouding everything in a tangible mist of vertical water.

And, as water often does once it's stopped being rain and turned into puddles — once the ground could soak up no more — it began rushing downwards. First into the brooks, streams, and rivers and then in torrents tearing through the woodlands, causing mudslides, and even uprooting less resilient trees.

All that water had to go somewhere, and as the lakes began filling up, threatening to break their embankments and then actually doing just that, it travelled ever downwards, creating new lakes and marshes on the way.

Those wouldn't last, no more than a few days or weeks or maybe even months in sheltered spots. But the valley's *actual* swamp — tucked away near a north-westerly corner — was already waterlogged and, unbeknownst to the two castaways, was now turning into a lake; a lake in which gnarled and leafless marshtrees now prodded through the murky, liquid surface like giant, grey stalagmites.

Erina looked at what the rain did to her "home" and thought 'drat!' Far away — though not nearly far away enough — others, too, looked at what they had, up until now, thought of as home.

The swamp was no more. And, with that gone, the inhabitants of the swamp left. The frogs didn't go far (if, indeed, they went anywhere at all). The fish, happy with the rapidly increasing size of their domain found new places to swim in. The apex predators of the swamp looked at their home and decided that this was *too* wet, even for their liking.

One pack sought refuge higher up. Turning their muzzles towards the mountains that rose up out of their beloved swamp, they began to climb. Their large pads served them well on the uneven ground.

After some serious arguments, and a few bites in all the wrong places, the two other packs, driven together by the rising waters, parted ways – one seeking solace in the pine forests nearby. They would wait, patiently, for the waters to recede again.

The last pack, the closest territories already claimed, either by their kin or by those even they dared not oppose, was driven the furthest. They didn't need to travel more than a few days' worth. But once they set out, following the shape of the floor of the valley, there seemed to be no reason to stop.

'As if things couldn't get any worse,' Erina huffed and aimed a kick at an innocent bit of debris. It wasn't the best thing to vent her frustration on, but it had to do.

It clanged complainingly and, before it flew off, stumped her toes. 'OUCH! MY FOOT!'

Hopping around on one leg, her face clouding over more and more, Josh hid inside the shuttle. He had no wish to get in the Cognitor's way, not when she was in *that* kind of a mood. He also didn't think it was a good idea to let her see him laugh himself silly at the sight.

The Cognitor might not seem as glamorous, or as scary, as she once had, but she still made him jump; whether it was by turning around and finding her suddenly there or the faces she made when annoyed. Also, her eyes creeped him out, the way they grew cold and distant when things didn't go her way.

There were further clanging and squelching sounds from outside, then Erina appeared, dropped the containers she'd been dragging back and, with an, 'I'm going out!' bark, was gone again before he had time to ask what was happening or stop laughing.

Now, Erina stomped through the forest like a reckless, but very localized, moving disaster zone, walloping anything that got in her face.

Normally, hitting things released some of that pent up frustration, but, seeing as most of what hit her back here were branches, filled with wet leaves, smashing them only came back around and soaked her in the process.

It took time before Erina's heart stopped thumping hard enough to break through her ribcage, or her veins to stop threatening to burst through her skin, they were throbbing so hard.

Anger never was one of her better mastered emotions. And, out here, far away from people, she'd let herself go in terms of controlling it. Maybe it was time she started working on that again?

Her footing constantly slipped on the now muddy ground. But she pressed forwards, splashing through the puddles and small gullets created by the storm.

They'd soon dry up, but, in the meantime, they were happily making life "interesting" for her. Much like she was doing for some of the forest's inhabitants. Though, in her defence, she didn't mean to.

'Sorry about that!' Erina called after one of them as the red flash of fur streaked up a nearby trunk after she'd almost stepped on its tail. It had tried to stay on the driest path. So had she. Still chattering at her, the squirrel disappeared amongst the branches.

She took a deep breath. Anger took a toll on you. Sometimes it filled you with dark energy. Sometimes it just drained you. You had no right to get so tired from just strolling through bits of greenery, she thought.

Erina looked at where she was for the first time since she'd stormed out of the camp.

'You know, I don't think I have the faintest idea of where I am!' she said, almost amused by the fact.

As Erina tried to work out where she'd ended up, the distressed squeals of something large and even unhappier than she was, reached her ears.

'Well, guess we'll leave the "where" for later then, shall we?' She tried to brush off some of the mud clinging to her lower self, failed, and set out to find what was making all that infernal racket.

It turned out to be … an old friend. And … something else…

'Yah! YAH!' Erina shouted and ran forwards, startling the vicious looking creature that leaned over the tri-coloured horse. Its fangs snapped shut on a large vine at the sound of her voice.

'Yah!' Erina bellowed again. 'Go on. SCRAM! You're not eating *anyone* today.'

The blue menace threw its head up in surprise, eyes wide. Dropping the vine, it snorted loudly, stamping and pawing at the ground with its spurred hooves. Tossing its horned head, it paced uncertainly.

When Erina yelled again, it whirled around. With a last lash of its spined tails against the vines, it was gone. She'd barely had time to take in what the thing looked like before the blue shadow had disappeared amongst the trees.

'And stay gone! D'you hear?' she called after it, slowing to a walk. 'What in the world happened to you?' Erina shook her head in disbelief, watching the tri-coloured horse before her.

He stayed quiet for a moment, but began complaining again as soon she reached for the vines that had trapped him.

'That's it. It's okay. It's okay. Easy. Ea-easy, fella,' Erina shushed him. She tried to keep as still as possible while also reaching out towards the ani-mal.

The stallion whinnied shrilly and tried to kick out, clearly unhappy. Erina would have been too, if she'd managed to get herself tied up like that.

The only thing he achieved by thrashing about was to get himself further entangled in the thorny bush-vines. How he'd gotten into them in the first place was a mystery. Erina just couldn't see the proud horse do something like shy from a squeak in a nearby bush, stumble, fall, and get caught like that.

'Did that nasty blue beasty chase you into this?' Erina murmured sooth-ingly, pulling at a thorny creeper.

It bent, but that was all. 'No leeway there then. Hmm… Guess cutting this is going to be the only way.'

Having salivating fangs snapping and snarling on his tail would explain why he hadn't been more careful about where he was going. But if he'd been chased by a predator, surely getting caught by the creeping creep would have given him a life expectancy of thirty seconds or so.

Erina glanced at the ground. There was a lot of dirt and mud churned up. Almost as if there had been more than one of them. There were some tufts of fur too. Grey fur. Strange. The blue menace hadn't looked the furry type. It hadn't been grey either. She shook her head, trying to steer her mind back to the task at hand, and pulled out a knife.

'Let's try this, shall we?' she tapped the hilt against her teeth.

Erina kept up a continuous monologue as she sawed through the surprisingly stubborn vines. The quadruped rolled his eyes at her, trying to turn his head to follow her motions. But, while he huffed, the horse stopped thrashing. He just laid there, sides heaving.

'Good boy.'

Slowing down and taking the time for him to get used to her presence, Erina took the opportunity to examine the horse closer.

Now that he was keeping more or less still, she finally had a chance to get a good look. It was the first time she was this close to him and, up close, he was still definitely a horse, no doubt about that (though Erina was pretty sure that anyone who knew their way around equines would argue about that).

But even Erina was pretty sure that "normal" horses weren't made up of swirling paint patterns that alternated between deepest black, stark white, and a fiery red.

It wasn't the "we call it red but it's really a sort of murky brown" either, but a deep, blood-coloured scarlet. It practically tried to gauge out your eyes.

If anything he looked like someone had taken one of the court jesters of old and magically transformed them into a horse. All he was missing were the bells and the jaunty cap, Erina chuckled.

On top of that, with a mane and tail that began in black and ended in white, he reminded her of a skunk too.

Keeping one wary eye on the sky, as the day was getting on and she really wanted to get back to the shuttle before it got dark, Erina was thankful when the vines, thorns, and brambles began giving up their prey.

'You know, for someone who sure puts up a lot of fuss when *I* get close, you certainly don't have any trouble showing up uninvited and stealing *my* stuff,' Erina told him as the stallion huffed at her again.

The bush-vines weren't just prone to sticking their thorns in you, ripping and cutting. They were terribly reluctant to come apart, resisting all the way up until they snapped unexpectedly, coiling back on themselves like rapidly retreating snakes.

'Maybe this would have been easier if they were dry,' Erina grumped. It was turning out to be harder than she'd expected.

But she kept hacking at the vines, trying to keep them from doing more damage than they already had, until, with a final kick and grunt, the tri-coloured horse broke free.

Stumbling on his first steps, vines and creepers still reluctant to let go were tangled in his legs. He stomped a bit. A shiver went through his lithe body. Then he just stood there, looking sorry for himself.

'So, not running away as usual then?' Erina asked. 'Guess you have some sense.'

Glancing downwards, she could see that the vines had cut into his fine-limbed legs and, while they didn't bleed much, he was clearly uncomfortable.

'You really *are* exhausted, aren't you? Poor thing. Let's see if we can't get you sorted out, shall we?'

Back "home", Josh had, for several hours, been absorbed by the delicate nature of the diom, carefully doing things like opening the back cover, teasing apart wires, staring at the tiny nano-like circuit boards through some seriously strong magnifying glasses, and rubbing his eyes a lot.

It had been great not having the cognitor under foot for a while. For someone so small, she sure managed to get on your nerves. He'd hoped that he'd get some real work done with her out of the way.

But it didn't seem to be helping. No matter what he did, the diom stayed dead, much like its previous owner. This was a rather depressing thought and Josh tried to push it down every time it rose to the surface.

So it was a tired and somewhat grumpy young crewman who finally stepped out of the remains of the shuttle and shaded his eyes to see better. 'Damn, the suns are bright,' he said. 'Wonder if there is anything to eat today? Getting sick of doing most of the cooking.'

He took a deep breath and stretched his neck until it went, 'crack.' It smelled warm and musky. He hadn't even realized the suns were so low. No wonder the world was starting to sparkle in red and orange.

Josh was, therefore quite surprised to see the cognitor returning to the camp. It was so late, he figured she must have returned hours ago yet managed to avoid making a sound. She could do that, when she wanted to, he knew.

This time, however, she wasn't returning alone.

For the barest of moments, Josh imagined they were saved. Then, deflated by the sight, he sighed. Now, why couldn't the cognitor have brought back a search party? At this stage, he'd even be happy to see a wounded rach. Any sign that they'd made contact with the outside world.

Ok. Maybe not a *wounded* rach, those things were vicious when cornered. Sadly, the new arrival was wearing neither suit, gear, nor any other form of clothing. Rescuing was apparently *not* on the menu.

Neither was he, judging by the lack of fangs. That was a welcome change.

Josh wondered if you could eat horse, but one look at Erina and he kept that thought to himself. He'd seen that expression before and had no interest in getting his ass kicked.

'Well, don't just stand there,' Erina told him as she managed to coax the strangely coloured horse all the way into the camp. 'Go fetch some ointments or something. And see if you can find some clean rags or something else to use. I'm sure we have some left … somewhere.'

'That's a … horse.'

'Yes, he knows.'

'What are you doing with a horse?'

'Wraps, Josh. Now!'

'D'you mean to use them on that?' Josh exclaimed, waving his hands in the direction of the horse, who didn't at all care for all the arms flapping about all of a sudden.

'Obviously,' Erina scowled at him.

'Why? What good will that do us? He's not gonna sprout wings and fly us out of here, is he?'

Narrowing her eyes, Erina managed to diminish him with a look despite being a whole foot shorter than he was. 'Wraps! Josh! Now!' she growled from between clenched teeth.

The tri-coloured horse was clearly not fond of all the fussing, but he was too exhausted to do much more than just stand there. His usually so vibrant red coat looked matted and tainted dark with mud. The long tresses of his mane where knotted, twisted, and filled with twigs and broken pieces of thorns.

It took some time to get him cleaned up, but, eventually, he looked vaguely like a horse and not like a mud monster.

By the time they were finished, he'd even perked up enough to start fidgeting again.

'Woah, easy there,' Josh called out as he narrowly managed to avoid getting trampled by the large stallion as he shifted backwards nervously.

Josh quickly scrambled out of the way.

'He don't look very grateful for what we just did,' Josh pointed out.

'He's a *horse*,' Erina said as if this explained everything.

While, that first day, their new quadruped friend didn't stay, as the days went by, Erina noticed that the horse would often be seen at the edge of camp. Not only that, but she'd see more of him when she was out and about as well.

Not only was he now comfortable enough to allow her close but, if anything, he was now sometimes a little *too* close.

'Hey,' Erina exclaimed. 'What do you think you're doing? You can't eat those.' She pushed away an inquisitive muzzle from where the dried weeds were smouldering.

It did give off a pleasant scent, but it wasn't *that* great, she thought.

Clearly not in the mood to be stopped, the horse tried to snuffle at it again. Touching the hot stuff caused him to shy back, almost stumbling over his four legs.

'I told you,' Erina chuckled. 'You do that, you'll get burnt.'

The horse snorted and tossed his long mane, narrowly avoiding setting it on fire.

'You know, I can't keep calling you horse.' Erina wracked her brains for a while. 'What do you think about Harlan? You kind of look a bit like a harlequin in a jester kind of way. Harlan. Harlan Illusion — because you keep disappearing on me!'

The newly-christened Harlan took no notice and tried to eat her hair.

With a bit more time, not only did Harlan grow used to even Josh's company, but they grew used to his. That was when they didn't randomly stumble over him snoozing somewhere. It seemed he had a talent for always turning up where the least expected.

'Aren't horses supposed to sleep standing up?' Erina heaved one time. 'Come on Harlie. MOVE, will you! I can't open the door with you blocking it like this.'

Despite a few setbacks like that, including those caused by the mischievous nature he showed in camp once he'd clearly learnt it was safe, Harlan soon proved to be more than merely good company.

Like when Erina left to go exploring in the world outside camp. Though it would have been even more useful if he'd actually carried something, bags, gear, even her, she was still very grateful for the company. She told him so. Rubbed his forehead and told him he was a good horsie. Scolded him when he stepped on her toes with those hard hooves of his. Chased after him when he stole something of hers and made off with it.

It was difficult to say if Josh was jealous or not. He certainly did end up being on his own a lot more than before.

Erina was kind of glad she wasn't, especially those days when they were out-and-about and that creeping feeling snaked down her back. She always tried to shake it off, but it often felt like they were being watched by eyes, many eyes. Eyes hiding behind every thorny bush, mysterious berry patch, and leafy trunk.

When Harlan was there, the local wildlife was usually content to ignore her. Occasionally, a lonely deer would scurry away into the safety of the forest. Other than that, the place seemed very empty.

But the feeling of being watched still persisted.

'You know. I always thought that forests and such were supposed to teem with life,' Erina confided in the tri-coloured — no, trias — stallion one of those times.

The horse merely neighed, shook his long silken mane, and cavorted happily around her as they reached a clearing. Dropping the satchels on the ground, Erina sank down beside them in the long, luxurious strands of softness. One of the blades of grass cut her.

'Ouch!' Erina sucked at the thin cut. That stung. This was tiring work, she thought. Painful, too.

'And it would go SO much faster if you let me ride you,' Erina told her companion as he pranced past her. 'You've got *four* legs, I'm sure you can spare some, can't you?'

But as much as Harlan seemed to love games, he wasn't playing that one. While he was happy to be petted and for her to tease brambles and other things from his mane and tail as she marvelled over the velvet feel of his coat, he put his foot, no hoof, down about that: No riding.

She had tried, once, and, while Harlan had been very good about it afterwards, it had been a pretty embarrassing experience as far as Erina was concerned.

Nimble enough, it hadn't been hard to convince Harlan to stand still long enough near a large rock, so getting onto his back had been easy. At which point he'd turned his head, gazed at her with a curious expression and then gone back to grazing.

Erina was quite sure that wasn't what was supposed to happen. When nothing she did made him move anywhere, she'd slumped forwards, sighing. As a result, she ended up, head-first, in some nearby bushes, when Harlan kicked out as something bit him on the rump.

When they'd crashed here, her equine knowledge amounted to being able to tell the front end of a horse from the back. But now, with Harlan, she was learning every day. It was slow going. She still had trouble telling apart an ear flick that could just as well mean, 'I want to but I'm not admitting to it, you go first,' as it could mean, 'I'm annoyed as hell and I'm not gonna to take this anymore.'

Now, both ears were pinned close to his skull. The frivolity had come to an end. Below his red, black and white hide, she could see powerful muscles quivering.

'What is it, boy? What do you smell?'

Getting to her feet wearily, Erina tried her best, but, to her, the glade looked like it always did. Where they were was hardly even worthy of being compared to a forest. The trees surrounding them were sparse and young and you could easily see a sky — so blue it almost hurt your eyes — peeking between their felt green crowns.

Erina sniffed the air experimentally, but it only smelled of warm flowers, grass, and that tad bit of moisture you got around some trees.

'Is it that blue beast again?' she asked.

The sky's bright earnestness was in stark contrast with the growing edginess of the two companions. They're right, Erina thought. Worry really *does* spread like a wildfire.

'Something's wrong.' Erina placed a hand on her companion's neck. Harlan fidgeted a little but didn't pull away from her touch. 'But I'll be darned if I know what it is. Let's get out of here,' she suggested, beginning to pull back the way they'd come.

Harlan remained motionless a little while longer, then, with a flash, the stallion whirled around and galloped off.

'Oh thanks, just leave me behind, why don't you?' Erina called after his rapidly disappearing tail.

Hidden deep in the shadows of the distant treeline, where the trunks grew a little closer together and the bramble reached up to meet them, something rumbled low and menacingly.

It followed the two companions with its yellow, unblinking eyes. Then, when certain they weren't going to notice it, it slunk back, padding away on silent paws.

CHAPTER SIX

'Suppose they *could* have packed something other than nutrilicious bars,' Josh said and bit into his with a sour expression.

He wasn't any fonder of the food cubes than Erina. No one was. They still hadn't had much success with making food that kept when travelling though, so it was either those or nothing.

'That's one mean inventor for you,' Erina agreed with a huff. 'Does keep you from wanting to live off them, mind you.'

'Who'd want to?'

'Exactly.'

For once, they'd both decided to spend the day together. They'd been out exploring during the day and had stopped for a well-earned rest — and lunch — by some innocuous looking rock piles.

At least, they'd assumed they'd been rocks from afar. Partially because most of them that were sticking out of the small hillock were worn down from wind and weather and had long ago begun to resemble their cousins from which they originated.

'You know, if this *was* a building once, wonder what it was?' Josh mulled the thought over.

'Not built of glass and steel, that's for sure,' Erina agreed. 'Harlan, stop that!' she pushed an inquisitive muzzle out of one of her pockets.

Looking insulted, Harlan returned to gambolling around them, whinnying. Old ruins were hardly fun and definitely not playful. They just sat there. They'd always just sat there like boring ducks bobbing on the water, except without the bobbing. He'd much rather play with his human.

'Big though…' Josh said after a while.

'There are other small hillocks around here. Wonder how many have buildings beneath them?'

'Think we found a lost civilization?'

'Hah,' Erina scoffed. 'The only ones lost around here are us!'

But showing more animation about something than he'd done ever since the crash, Erina eventually caved in to his enthusiasm. 'Okay, okay. We can poke about a bit longer,' she sighed. 'Not sure how useful it'll be though.'

Snorting at the lack of attention, Harlan drifted off. Neither human paid much heed. They were both much more interested in their new discovery — though Erina was going through great motions to pretend otherwise.

'This place must have been abandoned long before we got here,' Josh announced. He straightened up from pulling at tufts of grass and dirt and massaged his back.

'Way, WAY before we got here,' Erina agreed.

'This sure isn't as easy as you'd think.'

'Speak for yourself.'

Ignoring the jab, Josh continued investigating the ruins. 'Think this might have been a tower at some point,' he said after some further poking.

Up until this point, Erina had mostly considered him as just another pair of hands. How very uncharitable of her, she now thought. She still wasn't sure what use the knowledge would be, but anything that helped them recognize themselves in this lost world was helpful, after a fashion.

'Can you see any other small, raised mounds? They might hold more clues like this one.'

Josh jabbered away excitedly about what all this could mean. Meanwhile, Erina scanned the surrounding landscape and, sure, there were some more mounds scattered here and there. She shrugged. How could she tell the difference between a mound with stone under it or something crafted by the local mole population?

'This place. You know, I think it might have been one, single building,' he said after a few hours of poking and prodding. 'Look, maybe even with outbuildings on the sides and open courtyards within, around which the central structure was. Fascinating.'

'Fascinating?' Erina rolled her eyes. Her back was beginning to ache from all that looking down. She eyed him suspiciously. He even sounded different from before. He wasn't possessed by the spirit of some long-since-dead famous archaeologist or something, was he?

'I don't think we're looking at a natural landscape at all,' Josh said, eventually. 'Sure, there's bigger structures back home, but, you know, they've never found any ruins. Not a trace. Not a single trace of anything that came before.'

'What about the dragons? That crazy scientist must have found those remains somewhere,' Erina interrupted him.

'Bah,' Josh dismissed the idea with an irritable wave of his hand. 'Those are just rumours. I'm talking buildings. Structures. *Things*! You realize we might be looking at the only remains in the whole world of what was before *the Orion came here?*'

Blinking, Erina pulled back on her wish to throttle her companion. 'What?' she said, rewinding the last five minutes' conversation and scanning it for something remotely important.

She ran her hand over some of the now partially exposed stonework. Josh had worked furiously, albeit not very carefully, to unearth them. Somewhere back in time, an architect was weeping, she was sure of it.

Some of the stones had probably made up the foundations or lower levels of some bearing walls, because they were huge — even by her standards. If she stretched out her arms wide, she still wouldn't have been able to reach both ends at the same time.

'How utterly uninspiring,' was her scathing conclusion.

If Josh noticed, he didn't let it stop him. He continued to make observations out loud, forming ideas and creating castles-in-the-air, all the way home.

'I don't suppose it matters,' Erina confided in her equine friend later on. 'Ever since we found those ruins, he barely takes his nose out of them. Honestly, if I didn't know better, I'd say he was happier than I'd ever seen him before. Not that I actually ever usually *saw* him, you know, on the ship.'

'I just hope we one day don't run into something nasty out there.' Erina sighed again and patted Harlan's neck. 'You know, I'd feel a lot better if the blasters were working.'

Days had come and gone since they first stumbled across the ruined remains of The Valley's past. Neither of it was grey, but to Erina it felt depressing, even a bit like trespassing on a memory.

Now, she poked her head into one of the openings they'd managed to dig. It led further in. Further down. Erina wasn't too keen on the down part.

'What'ya see?' came from behind her.

'Nothing. It's pitch black in here. Hand me that torch, will you?'

'Maybe it would have gone better if you had stuck the torch in first?' Josh ventured hesitatingly.

Pulling back, Erina grinned roguishly. 'Where would be the fun in that?'

They spent some time shoving experimentally at the stonework, but whatever was going to collapse here had, well, collapsed, already.

'What'ya think? Some sort of storage area? It probably wasn't always underground, though the vaulted ceiling does suggest it could have been designed to be that.'

'They might have wanted to include a door, if this was some sort of reinforced root cellar,' Erina frowned.

Now that they'd dug through the small burrow, daylight was flooding into the antechamber. What lay beyond remained in darkness. There were traces suggesting that something had lived here, probably before the structure had gotten blocked off. Even back then it must have been pretty dark though, Erina thought. Whatever had used this as a lair, they hadn't been early risers by the looks of things.

'Nocturnal,' they guessed in unison.

'You don't strike me as a typical history buff,' Erina said, giving her companion an evaluating look.

Josh merely shrugged, taking another torch and preparing to head deeper inside. 'I guess I always liked all that "old stuff," you know? I wasn't gonna spend the rest of my life as a glorified floor sweeper on a planetary runt you know. I just wanted to get out there and see the sights.'

There wasn't much she could say to that. The *Random Star* wasn't huge, as ships went. And it was true that it didn't fly further than the outer planets — but then, neither did anything else. Though she was pretty sure the captain wouldn't have cared for his precious ship to be called a "runt."

'Is it just me, or are those bones awfully large for that small hole we dug out?' she mused, casting a suspicious glance over the accumulated remains in some of the alcoves.

'Older… I think…'

'As long as they're not here now,' Erina quipped. She'd always much preferred machines to animals. Not that they were, always, much better behaved, but, when a robo-dog misbehaved, you could just shut it off and stuff it in a cupboard until you took it to be repaired — or forgot you had it, whichever came first.

There were still shelves lining some of the walls back here. Definitely some sort of storage space then. She wrinkled her nose. She could have done without the smell.

It wasn't as much intense as it was persistent. The kind that invades your mind without having to bother about going via your nostrils. It gave you an urge to keep looking over your shoulder, just in case its owner was creeping up on you.

'Oh well, I suppose we could do worse,' Erina eventually admitted.

Josh didn't rise to the bait. It wasn't like there were a lot of options out here and just finding this place had been a stroke of luck.

It would make for a solid, non-leaking roof over their heads and they could scavenge something to use as a door from the shuttle.

'Wonder what happened to the people who built this?'

'Well, they didn't leave for sunnier climes, that's for sure,' Erina said. 'No one's ever found any trace of ancient civilizations on this planet. None. Zip. Zilch. Nada. Everything explored since the days of *The Orion*? Nothing. Not a trace.'

'Maybe they were all trapped *here*?' Josh mulled it over. 'If the world burned around them, maybe there was nowhere left to go?'

'Could be, Josh. Could be.'

While Josh was taking delight in unearthing new discoveries. Though this did indeed involve a lot of sweeping, much as his job had done on the *Random Star* — for some reason, he didn't complain about it.

Meanwhile, Erina shook her own handiwork. 'Well it doesn't fall apart. That's got to be something.'

She gave it another shake, just in case it had changed its mind, then pulled at the ropes. 'Seems steady enough. What d'you think, Harlan? Want to try it on?'

The trias merely snuffled at her creation. Then he reached out and nibbled at it.

'Hey you're not supposed to do that!'

Harlan's head jerked back at her raised voice — the makeshift halter in his teeth.

'Oight, get back with that,' Erina called out after the now wildly prancing and bucking horse.

She ran after him as he enjoyed his new toy. 'That's *not* a toy,' she cried.

But Harlan was having too much fun to pay any attention to his human. He tossed the bits of rope into the air with glee. Occasionally, he missed catching it and it fell on the ground. Then he'd buck, paw at it with his front hooves, and pluck it up, starting the whole circus again.

As Erina almost caught up to him, he shifted out of the way as she made a grab for the halter.

'Harlan! Do you have any idea how long it took me to make that,' Erina cried out despairingly. 'Give it back!'

The stallion snorted and let her — almost — catch him, then danced out of the way with a swish of a tail in her face.

'Harlan!'

After a while, he seemed to tire of the new game. Possibly this was because Erina was no longer chasing him around on the slippery grass. She'd sunk down onto the ground, on her back, spreading her arms wide.

Bored, Harlan trotted back to where she was to see if she could be enticed into some more playing.

Erina avoided growling at him as he dropped the, by now, ruined halter in her lap and instead tried to burrow under her arm like an overgrown puppy.

She shoved him away.

'Thanks for that. What are you? Some sort of overgrown dog? Suppose you'll try to wag your tail next.'

Erina sighed as she picked up the entangled mess.

'Maybe it can be salvaged,' Josh suggested meekly as he dropped the satchel he'd been using beside her.

Whatever was in there, it must have been heavy, because it went thud where it landed.

'I don't supposed there're more straps are there?'

'I don't think so, Cognitor.'

'Darn it,' Erina exclaimed. She aimed a small kick at a pile of the loose stuff. 'Ouch! Stupid crash site,' she growled. 'Can't you ever find something useful in this place?'

Ignoring both horse and human, she stomped off and was soon out of sight, not returning until several hours later.

It took several more tries before they, together, discovered a suitable solution to the lack of rope. And, after a lot of pulling and heaving and general banging on sheets and vents to find them, they eventually pulled out several long strands of data cables.

At least they assumed they were data cables. The things came in all colours and varying thickness and when you pulled at them you kept pulling out miles and miles of the stuff.

'We're finally giving up on ever making this fly again, then?' Josh wiped the sweat from his forehead.

'What do you mean, *finally*? No, don't answer that. Seriously, how much of this stuff can one single ship hold?' Erina stared at the pile they'd collected. 'I mean, don't you think there's more stuffing than duck here?'

Josh scratched his head. 'I don't know. Maybe they're bigger on the inside?'

'Hah, I wish,' Erina huffed. 'Come on, help me get these back.'

It took quite some time, but eventually they managed to get a useful bundle out of the mismatched cables. Plenty for everyday needs certainly, with enough material left over for what Erina had originally wanted it for.

'Is this really a good idea,' Josh asked again. 'I mean, how are we supposed to use the shuttle without these?'

Erina snorted. 'Come on now. Do you really think that it'll fly anyway? I mean, could *you* fix it?'

'No. But it could still hold useful information.'

'That's what the diom is for. And if you hadn't noticed, those aren't working either.'

'But still—'

'No buts about it,' Erina snapped. 'Now, if I do like this and then this and then pull, I should get something like … ah, voila!'

She held up a simple noose-like-thing that might, in a bit of a bad light, be mistaken for a halter. Now all she needed to do was to find Harlan. Apparently, while she had been busy working he had gotten bored and wandered off.

'Ungrateful bugger. Guess trying it on will have to wait until another day,' Erina sighed.

She was right. Indeed, it took several attempts and no small amount of fuss until the horse accepted the new, rather neon, accessory and even longer before he didn't pull away the moment he caught sight of something more interesting.

In fact, Josh made considerably more progress with his excavation, but, as Erina was quick to point out, the stones didn't wander off and get lost in the nearest bramble patch.

CHAPTER SEVEN

$\mathcal{J}$osh was busy and, instead of joining him in endless brushing of dirt — dirt wasn't interesting, except perhaps to grow things in, if you were good at that sort of things — Erina managed to coax Harlan into giving her a lift further out onto the plains.

She hoped he'd be around to give her a lift back home too. Otherwise, it'd be one long walk and she still didn't fancy the idea of spending the night out there, in the wild. Even if the most dangerous thing she'd seen all day today had been a very annoyed wildcat, which had hissed and spit at them from on top of the boulder where it had been sunning itself.

Since it had barely been twice the size of a rabbit, she hadn't felt threatened. Neither had Harlan who'd pointedly trotted past it with his tail swishing right over it, causing another hiss.

What stared at them *now* wasn't hissing. It was also bigger. A *lot* bigger.

'Nice doggie,' Erina mumbled, twirling her hands into the horse's mane. She could feel the muscles beneath her quivering. If Harlan decided to make a run for it, she certainly didn't want to get left behind.

The fur around the creature's muzzle was already stained red as it turned to regard them with cold eyes. The remains of its kill fell to the ground as, upon seeing them, it bared its fangs. A foot of sharp canines and enamel stared them in the face. Its whole body quivered as it began to growl. Half crouched, it moved towards them menacingly.

Head down, a curled upper lip in reply, Erina didn't make nearly as an intimidating sight.

Not only did she lack the fangs necessary, but she didn't actually, at the moment, wield anything more lethal than a knife.

'Oh crap,' she exclaimed.

The huge ball of fur and bristles leapt for her, missing her by inches merely because she dove to the side. Rolling under the massive body, she came up facing it as it landed, realized she wasn't there, and whipped around.

The trias stallion delivered a powerful kick to its body. Hard hooves met with calcium bones and the huge wolf creature yelped in pain and, momentarily, lost its footing.

That moment of hesitation, as it decided if it should go after this new enemy first, was all Erina needed.

'Bugger this. This is one battle I pick *not* to fight,' Erina exhaled, only now realizing she'd been holding her breath since the beginning of the encounter.

As the creature once more bore down on them, somewhere in the ensuing mingle of hooves, fangs, arms, and thrashing limbs, Erina managed to find her way onto Harlan's back again.

The stallion, already the colour of red blood, needed no further encouragement. Whether from surprise at the weight of a rider or because the rest of the pack chose that moment to make their presence known, Harlan took off as fast as his slender legs could carry him.

Behind them, for a moment clearly visible against the clear blue above the hill, came the rest of the pack. They flowed over it with deadly grace.

'Woah! Ow! Euow!' Erina cried out as she tried to cling on to the rapidly jigging and zagging horse, as Harlan plunged through a small copse and stretched out on the hilly plains.

In the woods, the enormous wolves' agility far outmatched his own. Out here, it was more even.

Erina risked a glance behind them. 'Oh great, now the whole bloody pack is after us.'

'Yah! Yah, Harlie!'

Not that Harlan wasn't already running at full tilt, but somewhere the lithe stallion found extra speed.

Up and down grassy knolls, the chase went. One moment their pursuers were almost upon them, snapping at their heels, the next they'd outdistanced them again.

Below her, sharp hooves thundered against the soft grass. Ears flat against his head, mane and tail streaming in the wind, Harlan raced for his life.

Catching wind of a large group of deer[9] — spread out in all directions and grazing placidly until the noise of the hunting party reached them — Harlan changed direction, making directly for them. The animals scattered, hopping and running, as he plunged right into the herd.

Braying and calling out to each other, the deerlike creatures took off as well.

For a moment, Harlan and Erina were mixed in with the herd, then the equine's longer legs and head start made him pull into the lead and then the deer were behind them.

'Those looked like good eating,' Erina mumbled as she clung on for all she was forth.

Those grey furballs must have thought the scattering herd made a good snack too, as, when Harlan began to slow down from the breakneck pace he'd set, they'd lost their pursuers.

'What the heck was that?' Erina asked the still nervous horse. 'It was the size of a house. Okay, okay … maybe not a *house*. A horse. But that's still big, for a dog. A very big, angry, alien … dog. Dark too, almost like a cast-iron pan.'

Taking care that she could check their surroundings, in case something else decided to pop by for dinner, the two of them rested, each with a wary eye on the horizon.

'Where the heck did they come from? Have you seen them before? No? We *are* a fair bit out,' Erina asked Harlan after a while, who merely nickered and tried to eat her hair in a friendly sort of way. 'But what if those we ran into aren't the only ones out there? If you hadn't been there, there's no way I would have been able to outrun them.'

Then it hit her. She had a horse. She'd been able to outrun them. Josh hadn't. He wouldn't.

'Oh dear. Harlan. This could be bad. This could be really, really bad!'

---

[9] Actually, they weren't deer at all, but Erina's grasp of exobiology was only marginally better than her interpersonal skills.

Erina bit her thumb and swung back onto the stallion's back. He was in motion even before she'd sat down.

It was probably safe to say that Josh's greatest worry right now was how he was supposed to convince the captain of the *Random Star* to let him take charge of the finds they'd made here. There was so much to discover. To learn. He'd had two things he'd really wanted to do in his life and space, the final frontier, hadn't turned out nearly as exciting as he'd thought it'd be.

'Turns out, all the *really* exciting stuff, was down here, all along,' he mused as he carefully traced the outline of a barely visible carving with his finger.

The stone was what Erina would have called a dull, uninspired grey, Josh thought. But the cognitor wasn't here now. He could work in peace and quiet for a change.

He'd already decided that what ruins they'd found earlier had just been the beginning of many. None of them anywhere near as sizeable, he was sure, but it was hard to tell when he could only get to the closest ones on foot.

But now that he knew there were others, he kept seeing them everywhere. Or the possibilities of them at least.

This one, it might have had inscriptions on it. Either that or it had been scratched at by something with really, really big claws.

The way of the new inhabitants of the planet was to be torn between an innate desire for the grandiose and a strong sense of keeping things functional. It had led to a building style that saw marble-ish halls, complete with ionic pillars, stand side-by-side with what could only be considered sugar cubes with a door. Neither would be grey.

In his mind's eye, Josh kept seeing the reception they'd get when they got back. He, alone, had found the missing piece of the puzzle they'd all been wondering over; how their world — a planet that must have been inhabited at *some* point — could show practically no trace of what had come before at all. Just a tiny fragment here, an infinitesimal piece there.

'Mind-blowing, really,' Josh said and sneezed when the sandstone let go of another layer of dust. 'I could get my name in the history books for this, you know.'

Nearby something rustled, derailing his train of thought.

'Stupid horse,' Josh mumbled, then remembered that the horse that had become so attached to the cognitor wasn't here. Neither was the cognitor.

Looking around, Josh froze. There, in the thicket, no more than a few metres away from him. A pair of bulbous, yellow, eyes.

The gaze held his, unblinking, as the shadows that had hidden it slowly, fuelled by his adrenalin gland, proved to never have been shadows at all.

What he'd taken for long strands of firm grass turned into a shaggy coat. A boulder into a body. The dark grey body of the largest wolf he'd ever seen rose from the murky innards of the crevice below.

Even standing on the bottom of the opening in the earth, its head was level with his own.

His hand went limp, letting go of what he'd been holding, and it clattered to the ground noisily. The creature began to growl, still deciding if he was another predator to be challenged or a very peculiar-shaped lunch.

Its head whipped around at the sound of gravel crunching somewhere behind. Josh didn't wait. He was already running when the dark grey mass of muscle and fur clawed its way up the sides of the gap.

There was a moment of rumbling. Silent paws on the earth. A flash of teeth.

When Erina eventually found her way to the scene, there wasn't much left for her to do.

What the iron wolves had left behind wasn't much more than some tattered bits of torn clothing and what looked like a cube of plastic gnawed and riddled with tooth marks. The plastic cube was approximately the size of a head.

'Helmet,' Erina guessed. She was just glad it wasn't *actually* a head.

The odd thing was, she couldn't recall Josh actually wearing a helmet. Maybe he'd brought it along from the shuttle for some reason?

There wasn't really much left to bury. But Erina gathered together what she could find, along with some of the possessions she knew he'd treasured. She also carefully buried an acorn just below the soil. Hopefully one day it'd grow into a big and strong tree. Something living seemed more fitting than just piling mere rocks on top.

For good measure, she planted some on the old graves as well. It somehow seemed like the right thing to do.

Then, once that was done, a great frown descended upon her brow. Her eyes turned to angry slits, glimmering dangerously.

'Right. Only one thing left to do now. Make sure those things never come back! When I'm through with them, their nth level descendants are going to… Big Bad Wolf? Hah! I'll show them. Just wait…' Erina growled.

But running off to fight hulking iron wolves with your bare hands was probably not the best idea, even she could see that. So, fuming with cold, calculated anger, she turned her attention to making sure it'd be a successful venture.

'Too bad I can't just shoot them. Guess we're going to need something a *little* bit bigger,' Erina scoffed and tossed yet another small, makeshift blade aside. 'Still, I do feel a bit bad — it's not like they're the local evil overlord, or something. Live and let live, and all that. But I draw the line at getting eaten.'

Surveying the stack of what might — in a pinch — be roped in as a weapon didn't exactly inspire hope (not unless they were attacked by bunnies with *very* soft teeth).

There were plenty of spears though, but she quickly put those aside. Her aim hadn't improved with those — despite practice.

'I suppose that's what you get in today's age. Not exactly much call for a small arsenal of galactic grenades when you don't actually have a whole galaxy to worry about.'

She wondered if there were something else out there beyond the stars. Being stuck in a single, lousy solar system wasn't exactly the epitome of exciting, she thought. Heck, even the first settlers had managed to traverse the stars to get here.

Admittedly, they hadn't done it on purpose. They'd meant to colonize a nice little planet a few hops, skips, and jumps away[10], not end up marooned on the other side of the frigging galaxy.

---

[10] Hops, skips, and jumps for your average interstellar stardrive that was.

'I can relate to that,' Erina muttered. 'Marooning is definitely overrated as an activity, Crusoe or no Crusoe.'

Pushing some of the smaller debris around with her foot, she tried to clear her head. She was resourceful, right? So, how about acquiring some resources?

'I don't s'pose you have a secret stash somewhere, do you boy?'

Harlan merely continued to graze. His long, black forelock fell fetchingly over one eye as he occasionally shook a fly away. He wasn't listening.

'Didn't think so,' Erina said. 'So…' she exhaled slowly through her mouth, '…it's down to getting creative. At last, something I'm actually *good* at.'

That was true. She'd always had a knack for breaking things in creative ways. Building them — now that was much, much harder. Thankfully, there were no sightings of the walking tooth armouries anywhere in the vicinity. It was probably too much to ask for that it'd stay that way.

'Maybe they don't come this far out from the woods?' Erina mused as she took stock of her accomplishments a few days later. 'Now, there's a bet that I bet wouldn't get very good odds. Not very good odds at all.'

The next morning, Erina again scratched her head. There were fresh tracks outside the remains of the shuttle again that night.

'It *looks* like it should just be one,' she said, brow furrowed. 'Suppose if it was one of the snarlies, there'd be a lot more scratching and biting. It's not like they'd take the hint that chewing through durasteel just doesn't work.'

She glanced over at Harlan, who sniffed at the tracks disdainfully.

'I bet you'd be a lot more worked up if it was a couple of iron wolves, too. Didn't seem to bother you, last night. Are you saying this visitor in the dark isn't someone we need to worry about? Or was it just because you were safe and sound *inside*?'

Blowing air from his nostrils, Harlan snorted and returned, yet again, to grazing.

CHAPTER EIGHT

'Stupid torrent,' Erina cried out, slamming her fist against the hull. She was bent double but still every gust threatened to blow her away like a leaf, tumbling her over the ground, over and over until she was nothing but a collection of black and blue and, possibly, both green, purple, and red too. The grass only covered the upper part of the ground here. If you dug down, you hit stone — worked stone at that.

Harlan had planted all four hooves on the packed earth, trying to dig down with claws he didn't have. His mane and tailed whipped like a frenzied huddle of snakes, stinging everything it touched.

The horse weighed a great deal more than she did, and he still had trouble. Bending his neck until his muzzle basically touched the ground, he huddled, wishing for shelter that wasn't there.

'I'm sure this isn't the season for this,' Erina complained at the top of her voice. The wind ripped the words right out of her lungs. They became lost in the howling.

Snorting, they both tried to press themselves into the ground — which was about the only thing that wasn't already in motion. Even the snow on the distant mountains was being tossed into the air and hurled far from home. It stood like a white mist around the proudest and highest of the peaks.

'Snowfell,' Erina whispered. She could swear some of the flakes melted against her cheeks after first stinging them with sub-zero chills. 'What are you up to?'

Harlan would much rather have faced the other way, turning his tail to the wind and just waiting it out. There wasn't much shelter out there — nothing to impede its progress as the weather front rolled in.

But Erina was determined to make them reach "home" before the storm got even worse. There was enough room for the stallion in the shuttle too, as long as he stayed in the middle and didn't startle over anything.

Far from Erina's location, even the iron wolves tucked their tails in and sought shelter from the cold, wet gales. Even with their massive paws, which gave them better purchase on the treacherous grounds of the marshes, they had trouble not getting blown away. This was one enemy they knew of old they should not challenge, could not defeat.

Once Erina and Harlan reached the downed shuttlecraft, they, too, huddled inside as the days rolled on by.

While the wind and rain pounded the world outside, they remained safe and dry, albeit, after that first day, not very happy. The air, with no filtration system, quickly grew stale (despite the many cracks), then fragrant — and not in the "dash of rose petal before you sleep" way.

When Erina and Harlan finally dared to poke their respective noses and muzzles out of the "house" it was with a sense of relief.

'Blimey,' Erina exclaimed, after having taken several gulps of fresh air. It tasted energetic and new — like air often did after a thunderstorm. 'And here I thought storms were supposed to *break* trees, not *bring* them,' she said, staring at the scene before them.

The landscape had changed. There was no other way she could describe what had happened.

The ground was in the same place, more or less, but there were now several sets of light, airy (and fully grown) trees close to the crash site — the kind perfect for leaning up against with a good book in the shade during the warmest part of the day, if you could read. If you didn't, it basically invited you to stand leisurely under it and occasionally swish a fly away with your tail.

Erina hoped it wasn't on purpose. Some sort of vicious scheme whereby, just as you were drifting away lolled into slumber by the gentle rustle of leaves in the wind, branches would whip down and tear your screaming carcass limb from limb.

She shuddered. A vivid imagination wasn't always a good thing.

A little further away, other trees now framed sections of previously open grassland. Not enclosing them, more like giving them a gentle reminder that they weren't wild any more.

Mostly though, they littered the place with trunks that looked like they'd been used as matchsticks by giants, hurled every which way and then some, and then forgotten. Some had been torn apart, reducing them to kindling barely held together by sheer force of habit.

Yet others had been uprooted, roots and all. Their crowns were massive even while slightly squashed. One she could see still had a bird's nest in it. Of the occupants, there was no trace.

Shading her eyes in the bright morning sunlight, she could swear the forest in the distance had crept closer. Still far away, it was now close enough that she could discern a tree trunk here and there, larger than the others.

Erina kept staring. 'Now that just doesn't make *any* sense,' she finally breathed.

She eyed the small stream that now bubbled happily, winding its way over what, in every way felt like, the "property." It even had fish in it.

'Where does the water come from?' Erina wondered, frowning. As if the appearance of such a water source made any less sense than anything else she'd seen this morning.

She sat down on a nearby, suspiciously rectangular, sand-coloured boulder and just gawped at it all.

Harlan merely flicked a curious ear a couple of times and then wandered over to the stream to get a nice, cool drink.

'This happen a lot here?' Erina called out to no one in particular. 'Redecorating nature, I mean?'

It would have been nice if someone had answered, 'Yes, why, every second Tuesday,' but the world remained mum on that front. It would have made it feel more natural (despite being unnatural in every sense of the word) if it was some sort of regular occurrence.

It was, however, very handy. Strangely handy, even. Suspiciously so.

Erina sighed, eyes narrowing as she scanned the surroundings for any clues to what might have caused this landscape upheaval.

'Apparently there's no end to the surprises in this place,' she muttered.

For a moment, she thought she saw something glittering, passing between the new treeline and the fields — like a shadow of golden light — but when she blinked, it was gone.

'Any chance of a wheat field or two? You know, for variety?' she called out, at random. You never knew: someone might be listening after all.

Not that she'd know what to do with something so agricultural. Erina had some vague idea that you started with seeds and ended up with nice, warm bread straight from the oven. But the process in between she was a little hazy on. It just felt proper to have some, swaying gently in their gold-coloured glory, that was all.

'Curioser and curioser,' she said.

It wasn't every day that you gained that by you staying in one place and the environs doing all the heavy lifting and moving. The new environment felt, Erina traced the word over her teeth, safe. Homely, somehow. Right.

She couldn't explain why. They just did. It wasn't a protective bubble. There was no border that, were you to cross it, the world turned different. But, somehow, it felt … protected. Even more so than the rest of the valley.

In fact, it was more The Valley. It felt, somehow, important.

Not that she realized it at the time, though, back in her mind, that small nagging voice that always kept a look out for the strange things out there, kept insisting that *something* had changed. It just didn't know what.

It lent a certain summery freedom to life.

If Harlan thought it was odd that his human companion was so carefree so soon after what they'd encountered, he didn't show it.

'You know, you could really do with a brushing,' Erina told the horse one day when looking up from preparing the sheath she was working on. 'You look like a bush.'

Harlan ignored her, content to keep cropping fresh lunch from the ground beneath. Occasionally, he'd prance around and some of his mane would get tossed away from his eyes before falling down and blocking his view again — as if his long, black-and-white forelock didn't do enough of that already. It nearly tickled his muzzle.

'I mean, look at you. You're such a handsome fella, and you're perfectly happy running around with burrs and the odd twig in your hair.'

It didn't matter how many she pulled out. How many times she straightened them out, combing through the strands until they flowed like silk through her fingers. There would always be more.

'I mean, what do you do? Roll in them when I'm not looking?'

But she did the best she could. The feel of the strands between her fingers was strangely soothing. She soon found herself drifting away, thinking of her time aboard the *Random Star*. About the events that had led up to her signing on on-board a stuffy, close-quartered spaceship where it was nearly impossible to avoid contact with other humans.

Looking at it like that, that decision hadn't made sense either.

She was Brought back to reality by Harlan, who'd turned his head and was now trying to, affectionately, eat her hair. Erina pushed him away, laughing. 'I don't know what I should do with you, you troublemaker you.'

It took a few more days — and a deep desire to eat something fresh — to push Erina away from her preparations and out into the Valley proper again. As she and Harlan travelled, it turned out that it wasn't only right where she lived that had received a makeover during the storm.

'At least the *stars* are familiar,' Erina mused as they glimmered above at night. 'Think I might have spotted a planet or two, too.'

The sky was brighter than she remembered. With no artificial lights to drown out the otherwise feeble light of the stars, they glittered in the dark vault of heaven. Except it wasn't dark. Blue and green, yes. Vast tracts were tinted purple, billowing like clouds, if clouds had had the patience to remain still for that long.

The nebula that bordered this tract of space might shield much of the rest of the galaxy, but it did make for impressive imagery. It was, however, a very familiar sight.

Turning over, Erina pulled the light blanket up to her ears before sleep claimed her.

'This place just keeps getting weirder and weirder,' Erina announced the next day, brushing some of her unruly hair out of her face.

They'd followed a likely looking stream for a while, meandering through the wooden patches and glens, before even realizing there was something off about it. Now she stared hard at it, as if trying to will this particular piece of H2O to start behaving as normal. It didn't.

Erina shook her head. 'I didn't know water could do that,' she said, a note of despair to her voice. 'You know, normally, there's this little thing called gravity.'

The stream didn't care about normal. It continued to flow quite happily — upwards.

Whistling for her companion, who'd wandered over to investigate a particularly interesting leafy bush, she still had trouble believing what she was seeing. Even with all the travelling she'd done in the solar system, apparently there were a few surprises left.

Shaking her head, she managed to pull herself onto the stallion's back with some effort. Guiding him, they continued to follow the stream's course. Since it was flowing upwards, logic dictated that its source should lie below them, somewhere. What she was interested in was where it was going.

Not that she held on to any firm belief that this place believed in logic. It *seemed* to follow all the normal laws of science. For instance, the vegetation didn't try to grow upside down and the rocks didn't suddenly have moments of existential crises and stopped being solid. But when you started looking at things, really looking at them in detail, you realized that while, individually, everything made sense, it was when you put it all together that it would have made a geologist, botanist, or any number of people whose professions ended in "ist" furrow their brows and promptly announce, 'This is impossible.'

In short, the environment around the Valley shouldn't be there and the different ones certainly shouldn't be in such close proximity to each other.

'I suppose I should be happy there aren't palm trees growing happily five meters away from a glacier. Or *on* it,' Erina sighed.

No. It was more subtle than that. That way you didn't notice it at first. Then, when you did, your eyes opened and you began seeing it everywhere.

Flowers that even Erina would swear were from different temperate zones, even different parts of the world, could be found in the same forest — blending in like camouflaged iguanas amongst the verdant greenery.

And the water, there was far too much water — streams, rivers, even tiny lakes — considering the amount of rain.

'It can't *all* come from the mountains,' Erina mused. 'It never rains much up there either — or snows, or hails or whatever it does. So, where does it come from? And where does it go?'

That was another mystery. Judging from the amount that flowed here and there it should have collected at the bottom of the Valley, filling it up like a giant reservoir.

Now, she wasn't trying to breathe the stuff, so it obviously had to go somewhere. But where?

Right now, she felt that was one of the more sensible explanations she could come up with. Erina liked explanations, they sorted the universe into tiny bits that could be understood and, thereby, supposedly, controlled … by someone, even if that someone wasn't her. She preferred it when it *was* her.

Erina clucked her tongue disapprovingly, resulting in Harlan picking up speed.

'Woah, slow down you maniac. I didn't mean *you*,' Erina cried out as the sudden jolt into a trot threw her off balance. Harlan tossed his head as she pulled back on the reins. He evidently didn't see a reason to take it slow on this, fairly well-travelled, path next to the watercourse, even if she did.

'Just because you know what's on the other side of the bend doesn't mean I do,' she told him pointedly as they continued down — or was it up — the path.

At least, it was as close to a path as any she'd seen so far, meaning it was little more than a shortcut shared by the local wildlife.

Pulling her eyes away from the ground, they once more came to rest on the horizon which glimmered through the trees every now and then.

'More mountains. Why is it always mountains? I mean, how many blasted mountains can you fit in such a small space?'

And that was another thing. They always looked like they should be days, if not weeks, worth of travelling away, yet, a few hours later, she'd be looking at their foothills (those that didn't just rise like straight cones of rocky wall bursting out of the tufts of grass, that was).

'It makes no sense,' became an often repeated mantra as the days on the "road" turned into weeks. 'It's as if there's only that much space to be filled, but it's somehow only big when you're an outsider or when it "wants to be."'

It wasn't as if the world helped you travel somewhere faster either. Not like a ship that just increased speed until the scenery went "swoosh, swoosh" past the nearest viewport.

When you looked about, at any time, you were always where you should be. There was just a small nagging voice deep inside her that insisted she shouldn't have been.

Sometimes the scents lingered too; so that you brought with you the smell of pine needles into a leafy glade, summer berries into a deep cave, or even the fresh scent of clear water, far from where any of those were actually present.

Too soon, yet not, the stream increased speed and the track led them around a very small waterfall, 'At least here you have the decency to fall downwards,' Erina muttered as they walked by, turned around a large moss-covered boulder, and stepped into a vista taken almost straight out of any tale of old ever told.

'Wow,' Erina breathed, eyes growing large as tea plates. 'When did I die and move to fairyland?'

Before her, the pale waters of an elongated lake gently lapped against a collection of pebbles and small shells, stirred only by the faintest trace of a breeze and the leap of a large fish or two.

Erina could see smaller, more colourful fish dart about on the rocky bottom from where she sat. It was so shallow here, she could have ridden out half a mile and still be no more than knee-deep, she thought.

On the opposite shore, pines and more leafy trees, like willows and maples, hovered precariously on a steep slope. One way, the waters disappeared into the distance. In the other, it was swallowed by a bend, out into which a heavily tree-covered ridge protruded.

In the air, there hovered a faint mist. As the sun shone but faintly through it, dispersing its light like a frosted night light, it looked like the home of every magical being she'd ever read about. It felt like it too, an almost prickly sensation on her skin.

It even smelled differently. Like something was hovering in the air, unseen, yet present. The scent of promises and light and, just possibly, what you'd think magic would smell like if you didn't know it.

From somewhere above came the cry of a hawk.

It was the first call of a bird of prey she'd heard since they'd crashed. Even if there had been specks dancing in the wind, amongst the clouds, on some days, they'd been too far away to see or hear.

Erina shook her head and blinked, still not sure if she was believing what she was seeing.

Her shuttle "home" was unnatural (considering how it had come about that wasn't so surprising) yet looked perfectly sensible. This place felt all natural but had around it the aura of wonder that you only found in a very few places on any world.

'If a unicorn stepped out to drink, it would fit right in,' Erina whispered. It was that kind of place. Where you barely dared to raise your voice, lest it'd destroy everything.

Until now she'd thought that, once you got past the central grasslands, wherever you went everything was made up of trees. Every surface was covered with them. Or there were shrubs. Okay, rocks too.

'Looks like I was wrong,' she breathed, awed by the sheer force of presence she felt here.

She slipped from Harlan's back and knelt down to take a sip of the cool, clear waters.

The horse put a hoof forwards, as he sought waters further out, scattering a whole school of tiny fish.

It turned out to be a good place to fish: once you'd overcome the sensation that you should tiptoe through the world, holding your breath reverentially. Though Erina still half-expected an elf, or a unicorn, to step out of the forest at any moment, it slowly became more real around her.

True, the fish didn't bite too well in the beginning. But once she'd cottoned on to the idea of using bait, it got a lot better and soon she had a steady supply of fish. Though she quickly decided that it was just as easy to get tired of fish as it was rabbit, which was nice enough, if you were good at catching them and didn't eat them too often. Erina usually expended more energy on them than they were worth and any larger prey, like say, some of the deer-like creatures, skittish as they were, still needed more skills than she had at the moment. Unless traps counted. She was good at traps.

While her first instinct in an argument was to bash the other person over the head until they agreed with her, animals weren't exactly willing to stand still long enough, looking dumbfounded and unwilling to believe she'd actually hit them. No, they were off like a shot the moment they even scented the suggestion on the wind that she wanted more than just to admire them from afar.

Fish were easier. After all, you didn't actually need to be right up close to catch some.

It was a shame the misty lake was so far from the shuttle "home" that she had to camp out here before heading back the next morning. It was hardly the first time, but it still made it hard to sleep at night. On the other hand, it did mean she got to enjoy white trout roasted on a fire, so hot it nearly toasted her fingertips too when she picked out the succulent white meat from the hardened, black shell.

It smelled wild and free, sitting there, occasionally threading another fish on a stick. Once you'd gotten the hang of how to clean them, the rest was comparatively easy, she thought.

'I couldn't eat another bite,' Erina said eventually, putting down the remains of the last grilled fish. 'Guess you don't want any?' she called out to the trias, who was leaning restfully against a nearby, leafy trunk.

The world seemed almost at peace.

She should have known it was too good to last.

In the bushes behind her, something cracked.

Erina whirled around, grabbing a stout branch in the process. 'Blast. The smell of the grilled fish must have attracted it. Harlan? Harlan where are you? Shoo. Shoo!' Erina flailed at the shadow amongst the trees with the wooden "weapon."

She couldn't see exactly what it was, but it was big, and she'd caught a glimpse of pearly white fangs and orbs of redness.

She'd seen those before. The snarlies had yellow eyes. The shadow in the forest, theirs was red.

'Go away! GO on. Scram!'

The stick wasn't really very sturdy and probably wouldn't have done her much good if whatever it was that was hidden in the brambles chose to attack, but, surprisingly, nothing happened.

After half a minute of nothing, Erina strode forwards, eyes narrowed and muscles tense.

Nothing. She poked some of the bushes. 'Nope, nothing there either.' Scratching her elbow thoughtfully, she tried to come to terms with that she'd actually scared it off.

'Great. Now I'm being stalked by that big blue menace? Wonder how you go about trying to not look edible? Is this *your* doing?' she waggled a finger in the air.

Lately, she'd caught herself in the habit of talking to the Valley as if it was alive. She wasn't, however, having much luck in house-training it.

CHAPTER NINE

There was little warning, not even a telling shift in the air, before the attack.

Back at the shuttlehome, Erina and Harlan had been resting, getting ready for another search of the Valley for the iron wolves, as Erina had dubbed them. It was also a good time to work on, and improve, the small set of bladed weapons she had amassed, some of which were even beginning to feel useful.

It was always going to be a matter of time, but Erina hadn't expected that the large predators would find her home so soon. Why they were even bothering, seeing as she didn't exactly make for standard menu fare for them, was beyond her understanding.

One moment, the two of them were making their adopted home ready for the night, a red dusk coupled with a steadily increasing breeze suggesting that securing the site and themselves for the night would be a good move. The next thing they knew they were knee-deep in flashing teeth, raised hackles, and several large, furry bodies.

'Blast!' Erina exclaimed as she rolled out of the way of a swipe from an enormous paw. It missed her but only just.

Another of their assailants, she saw, as she came out still in a rush, had placed itself between her and Harlan. The door into the shuttle was behind her, several metres to the left.

Except there wasn't any opening there. Since no one had expected the company of huge things with teeth, no one had thought to leave the door open either.

The third, and largest, of the beasts was pacing further out, cutting off the equine's main means of escape — open space.

'Been spying on us, haven't you,' Erina snarled. The creature towering above her returned her growl with one of their own, muzzle quivering.

Close by, Harlan squealed and kicked out at the nearest fur-covered face. It didn't connect. But the iron wolf did withdraw a few metres, teeth bared.

For a tense moment, the two groups remained locked in a stand-off. A feint here. A rush there. Then withdrawal.

They were being sized up. Erina could feel it.

She wanted to rush at them. She wanted to sink her teeth into their ruffs and shake them until they whimpered and ran away with their tails between their legs. Unfortunately, the only thing that'd accomplish would be getting her killed.

'Stupid instincts. Couldn't you do something useful? Like finding us a way out of this mess?'

Somewhere, in the back of her mind, Erina wondered if there was something that'd make the furry assailants back off. Something trivial and easily overlooked. But all she got was a white wall of nothing. No suggestions. Not even the whisper of an idea.

Pacing in front of her, the iron wolves snapped at each other, almost as if they were still deciding who got the honour of the first kill. She could feel the ground shake every time one of them rushed them, then broke off at the last second.

Then, suddenly, one of the iron wolves pounced. Several hundred kilos of muscle, fur, and bony spikes, threw itself after her. Erina slid out of the way and it collided awkwardly with the hull of the shuttle. The metallic noise rang out. An odd echo to the more primordial scene.

Between them, Harlan and Erina were clearly outnumbered. Outmatched. The wolves knew it. She could see it in their eyes.

She risked a glance to where her new not-sword rested. Darn it. Too far away. She'd never make it if she ran for it.

For the next moments, there was nothing in the air but the sounds of battle. It was hard to concentrate. As from a great distance, she heard Harlan's angry screams. The wolves' deep bass snarls. It was all growing fainter.

Then, yet another body entered the fray.

Even in the midst of the battle, Erina could tell the new arrival towered over Harlan but not the wolves.

Realization dawned. 'So *that's* what you look like up close,' she breathed.

Rippled with muscles, yet lean, she'd always assumed he'd be blue all over. She'd also assumed, if something like this came to pass, that he'd be joining their attackers.

She'd been wrong.

For starters, what black there was, made up large, flame-like markings all over his body. The body itself, which reared and lunged at the wolves, was a dusky blue.

'Someone's been eating too many rabbits,' Erina sniggered, even in the midst of the chaos.

The elongated equine head bit down on an iron wolf that had gotten too close. Long, thick canines dug through the creature's wild fur and drew blood. Another raked its fangs against the blue menace's rump.

With a guttural shriek, the unreal creature whirled around, spiked reptilian tails raking across a vulpine muzzle.

While they were all busy, the wind around them was picking up. A whirling rosebush tumbled past, burying its thorns in an unwary muzzle. Torn up bushes, loose shrubs, and leaves slapped into the hull with wet smacks. Gravel, dust, even smaller stones were getting picked up and tossed around.

'Ouch!' Erina yelped, a piece of shrapnel scraping her cheek.

A powerful gust tore through the field, causing the dark shadow to stumble and strain against the wind, as if something around his form caught, like a sail in a storm.

Still trying to leap, one iron wolf was pushed back by a combination of gusts, hooves, and something that couldn't quite be seen. Another whined, thorns the size of a man's hands pricking its sensitive nose.

Somehow the world was turned upside down. Predator turned into prey. Teeth met claws. Claws met fangs. Hooves, bones. And, between them, the two equines (as different as night and day they might be) managed to drive the attackers back.

The wind was now doing more than just picking up. It was howling. Again. How much stupid wind could there be in one place, Erina couldn't help but wonder, even in the midst of everything.

'Into the shuttle,' Erina yelled. She couldn't tell why she did it. It wasn't likely that either of the two out there could understand her. 'If we stay here, we'll get blown to smithereens!'

Shielding her face, Erina tried to pull the main doors shut. 'Bloody electricity,' she cursed. 'MOVE!'

For a moment, the shadow hesitated, then — as if choosing the lesser of two evils — it dove through the doorway as Erina managed to yank the doors shut behind them.

There were bangs against the hull as the wolves tested its strength. They lowered their muzzles to the ground, trying to stay upright in the ever increasing howl around them. Paws the size of dinner plates dug into the earth to avoid being toppled over and blown away like leaves in an autumn storm.

'Safe from the wolves, for now,' Erina breathed out. Looking about, there really wasn't much room to move. 'Well, isn't this just cosy,' she muttered sarcastically.

Two equines and a human bumped into each other as they tried to find both space and footing in the already cramped, dark space that hadn't been designed with their shapes in mind even when it had been fully functional.

Tearing off the safety of a glow stick, Erina tossed it to what served as a floor (it was downwards these days, hence it was a floor).

'My, what big teeth you have. You're not gonna bite me with those, are you?' she said.

Her eyes slid appraisingly over the newcomer's fangs, stained with red, to the sharp talons that grew out of his hooves.

The blue menace swished his snake-like tails nervously. Trying to find a corner of his own, it looked like he was about as happy about this idea as the rest of them.

Erina shrugged. 'Circumstances really *do* make for the strangest bedfellows, don't they?'

They all wedged themselves into whatever space they could find, as far away from each other as possible.

'I don't suppose you care to tell me your name? Do you even have one? I can't keep calling you a blue menace, now can I? What do the rest of your herd call you? Are they going to show up here too? What on earth *are* you?'

As Erina's heart stopped pumping adrenaline through her veins, her head, previously so cold and clear, was becoming muddled again with everyday thoughts. The snark just came along for the ride.

With the three of them cramped in there, it did indeed prove to be a long night. A night where they kept being buffered by fierce winds, strong enough to even manage to rock the shuttle, despite the lower half being partly buried in the earth.

It didn't allow for much rest. There was nothing like a floor threatening to become a wall to make you try to sleep with one eye open. Sadly, that was a skill she'd never acquired, so it was with yawning that Erina greeted the next day into being.

As light filtered through the one, unobscured viewport, it became evident that the two equines had settled their differences, had they ever had any, and were now nibbling at the base of each other's necks.

Harlan would still shy away, his ears pinned, when the other made any fast, unexpected movements, but otherwise they seemed quite chummy to Erina's eyes.

As she forced open the doors and the three of them stepped out, the differences between the two horses became all the more evident.

'And I'm calling you "horse" because I have no frigging clue what you actually are,' she told the newcomer as she ran her eyes over him.

'And what on all the earths are those things sticking out of your sides,' she asked, just noticing them. The same dark blue as the rest of him, they'd been camouflaged against his hide. 'They don't look useful. Do they hurt?'

If anything, they looked painful, she thought. Like large, bulbous lumps, thicker near the shoulders and then thinning out towards the rump.

'One thing's for sure,' Erina said, a small chuckle escaping despite everything they'd just been through. 'I'm sure not riding *you*. The last thing I need is a spike up my backside.'

She was referring to the line of bony spikes that ran all along the creature's spine and primary tail. Erina shook her head. 'Well, let's see what mess the weather in this place has landed us in this time, shall we?'

The iron wolves were gone. They had most definitely not left the camp as they'd found it. If there was something they *hadn't* ransacked, before or during the skirmish, the wind most certainly had dealt a final blow.

Shaking her head at the mess, Erina instead turned to the newcomer.

Now that she looked closer, the odd things on his sides appeared to be some sort of bony protrusion, covered by a thin layer of velvet, bursting through the skin, like the growing antlers of an elk. It felt downy to the touch, but the shape reminded her more of the bleached skeletons of dead birds.

The strange horse didn't seem to be bothered by them though, so Erina left them alone. Though maybe "horse" wasn't quite the right term. He certainly was equine enough, but no matter how you looked at it "horse" simply didn't conjure up an image of blue and black, spines, fangs, and claws.

'So, think we'll have any more unexpected guests, do you?' she asked as Harlan nuzzled her elbow, pushing it out of the way, trying to dig his head under her arm.

'Easy there,' Erina scolded gently. 'Are you *sure* you weren't a dog in a past life? Sit? Sit! No? Ah, well … It was worth a try.'

After some obliging scratches, the trias was content to rip into some fresh grass, still wet from the morning's dew.

They didn't see any signs of the strange visitors that had attacked them for several days. Then, after four days had passed, they heard the howls.

Guttural, deep, and reverberating, the sounds rang through the clear night sky. It was enough to send shivers through anyone's spine, including those who didn't have one.

Erina merely gritted her teeth. Her eyes narrowing dangerously, she slapped the last of the tools she'd been able to make into the new satchel.

'That's it. We're all set. I've had enough of hiding out here in the nothing. If this stupid world wants to throw towering monsters in my face, I'll be darned if I'm going to just stand here and let it. Let's find them first. And make sure they never, ever bother us again,' she snarled for the second time.

This time, she really meant it.

CHAPTER TEN

Their journey to find the iron wolves — or snarlies as she called them when she thought their actual name was too much of a mouthful — took them farther than they'd ever gone before.

Across the plains they rode. Around lakes and lochs Erina had never even knew existed, some which looked like they could well have a monster or two dwelling beneath the surface. Over treacherous stone and still waters. Through forests and trees filled with dancing lights. Past strange monuments and stone-circles from days gone by.

Erina and Harlan didn't travel alone. While not exactly together, their honestly peculiar, mysterious friend seemed happy to gambol around them as they plodded along. Sometimes, he'd return bearing gifts.

Erina preferred it when he didn't. Not everyone *liked* having half a stoat dropped in their lap. If he noticed her disapproval, it didn't stop him from doing it again.

'You're one strange fella, aren't you?' Erina played with the piece of grass in her hand. 'I seem to have acquired one dog and one cat, except both are horses yet they're not.'

But no matter how far they went, the only true trace of their quarry was their absence. Once or twice they caught faint howls on the wind, though that could just as easily have been the breeze passing through a rock formation way, way out of sight. This place seemed to collect locales like that. No, there was no way this was a natural setting, was there?

There were plenty of wondrous beauty spots to stop by to admire though. Not wanting to push any of them too hard, Erina made sure they took plenty of breaks.

Now, she pulled out of where her thoughts had been playing as Harlan nipped her on the arm. 'Ha-ha. Sorry. How's that, boy? You like that?'

Erina laughed when Harlan arched his neck to snuff at the wet cloth bag she was using to slosh water all over his back.

It was a hot day and getting doused in cold water from the stream certainly felt good for her. She figured Harlie would feel the same. She'd been right.

They were both standing in a shallow part of the stream, just where it widened enough to be more than just a trickling brook and you'd have needed very big legs to step across it in one go. Not that either of the equines were bothered, they just jumped. 'Very unfair,' Erina had pouted the first time she'd seen it.

The trias whinnied, shaking his head to dislodge a persistent fly.

'Okay, okay,' Erina chuckled. 'I should stop daydreaming and get back to work cooling you down, is that it?'

She watched where they'd ended up taking their customary noon break. It was, in a way, inviting, in a bleak sort of way.

'It's a shame we can't go swimming, isn't it, boy? Wouldn't that be nice? Maybe some other time. It's too hot to go very far today, anyway.'

Harlan must have thought so too, for he splashed in a circle around her, while the blue menace looked like he was alternatingly wondering if they were both crazy or if there was room for him too.

'You know, you're really, really scarlet red, aren't you?' Erina said, dripping some more water over her friend. 'Well, *most* of you.'

Sure, most of his coat blazed the screaming red of blood, but his legs were painted with a mix of black and, while the water turned his coat almost as dark all over, when it dried, it revealed that the upper part of his back and spreading out once it reached the rump, was black as well. It didn't break completely, just faded into red.

Tossing his head again — apparently, he didn't like water splashed on his ears — the long, almost silken, mane ruffled adoringly. She longed to braid her fingers in there, quietly working out the gnarls and knots.

His mane, too, started black, but turned to white closer to the tips, just like his tail, which was quite the sight when you saw it streaming in the wind, carried proud and tall.

Erina looked back and forth between her two equine companions. They weren't quite as different as night and day, but it was close.

'You know, we really need to think of a name for you,' she told their new acquaintance. 'I can't keep going around calling you "hey you," now can I?'

It took two more days before she finally settled on something, and then having to start over again since he refused to listen to it. Eventually, they compromised. If she made a sound he enjoyed, he seemed willing to consider it a name. Erina wasn't sure if, back in the world, any world, "Mordjen" actually meant something. If it did, she hoped it didn't refer to something cute and cuddly.

Much later, the small group came to a halt on a ridge. Erina swung one leg over Harlan's bare back, now sitting in an — albeit unsecured — side-saddle and began pulling things out of her satchel.

'Don't move, okay Harlie? There's a good boy.'

She clenched the stylus between her teeth while pulling at a tube of plastic. It unrolled on her knees, proving to be a makeshift map of sorts. Turning it around until it faced the same way they did, Erina studied where they were. Or, at least, where they were in relation to where they'd been. She needed to fill it in as they went.

'This map that Josh helped me make is really handy,' she confided in the horse. 'It was a good thing the actual survey map of the planet was blank on the backside. A good thing they had a hard copy too.'

She clicked the stylus against her teeth thoughtfully. Harlan snorted and shifted his weight.

'Harlie! I said *don't* move!'

Erina clutched at everything in her hands while grabbing at a tuft of mane to keep from falling off.

The stallion took a few steps, eyeing up a clump of shrubs and herbs that looked, to Erina's eyes, identical to all the other ones around them, and started to munch them contently.

Having to turn the map again, she muttered darkly under her breath.

She'd started small and explored more and more with time. The map, which had been almost blank, had grown complex and, often — partly because drawing wasn't one of Erina's best skills — a little unreadable.

At the sides, there were space for scribbles: observations and drawings of things she'd seen, like animals, birds, and plants. Strange rock formations and even weirder things.

They were, often, different from those in the world outside. Rocks were still, mostly, rocks. Granite hadn't suddenly acquired the ability to fly or anything like that. And while she understood it had only partial things in common with the stone those early — unwilling — colonists had named it after, it was still only stone.

She wished they hadn't insisted on naming stuff after other things they were familiar with. It would make any potential, future visitors from Old Earth very, *very* confused, she was sure of it.

For that matter, it made *her* confused.

It was bewildering enough when reading history books. You had to remember not to let the mind conjure images of what you were familiar with. Annoying, that's what it was. Why have the same name for three different things? It didn't make sense to her.

Mordjen trotted over, catching up with them at his own pace, and decided to inspect the fluttering piece of plastic closer.

'Whoah! Easy there,' Erina called out as his inquisitive muzzle brushed past, nearly unseating her.

His teeth caught the map and a small tug of war ensued.

'BAD horse!' Erina ducked as a facial horn swung precariously close. 'Let it go. LET GO!'

Giving a small kick in protest, Mordjen pulled away.

'How is anyone expected to work in peace in this place?' Erina grumbled. She settled a bit more comfortably and started comparing the map to what she could see.

She doubted she'd ever get used to how, when "common sense" told her something should go *this* way, it went *that* way, almost as if out of sheer contrariness. Usually that was her job. And if you started assuming that it would, it stopped.

It was enough to drive anyone mad, it really was.

'Right. So, if we're here,' she burned her eyes into the map, 'then *that* should be over there. It doesn't, you know, move with the seasons or anything? This place *has* seasons, right?'

Harlan merely took a few more steps, having apparently exhausted whatever it was that was so special about that clump. He didn't know what she was talking about, but the constant murmuring sounds were quite comforting, as long as she didn't raise her voice.

'Judging by the longitude and latitude of where we "should" have crashed, we "should" be having autumn here. Obviously,' she eyed all the verdant fields and forests, 'we don't.'

'I'm beginning to feel "should" is my new least favourite word,' Erina made a wry face. 'If winters here are anywhere near as unpredictable…' she shuddered at the thought of being buried under several metres of snow. 'Anyway, back to work.'

It was hours later when, by chance, Erina happened to look in the right direction and spotted something next to the narrow trail they'd been following for what seemed like ages.

'That looks suspicious, don't you think?'

She steered Harlan towards the broken branches: an idea he was not too keen on. 'Stand still. I can't see anything with you hopping about like a crazy mouse with the hiccups.'

But the trias kept fidgeting, making it difficult to get a closer look.

'Something came through here alright. Something big,' she said, her hands brushing against the torn leaves.

Erina shuddered involuntarily. The path before them was barely a path at all, but something had forced its way through. Something that had left tufts of grey fur clinging to broken branches, even small trees.

'Looks like we hit the jackpot, boy,' she said, sliding off Harlan's back when the horse refused to move forwards despite her urgings.

Most of the ground here was covered in shrubs and ferns, but, disappearing into the deep forest, there were footprints. Pawprints, really.

Well, *one* pawprint anyway.

It wasn't very reassuring. Big, heavy, and clearly suggesting whatever had made it had had some pretty big claws, it sat there like a fat reminder that its owner was something that could prey upon bears. Angry bears.

Were there bears here? She hadn't seen any. But she hadn't seen an iron wolf until one decided she'd make a nice snack either, so that didn't mean much. And where you found one iron wolf, you found others.

'They definitely came through here.' Erina rummaged in her shoulder bag before pulling out a small plastic jar.

She shook it vigorously, then twisted the top until it came off in her hand. Pulling out a thin, white strip, she touched it to the imprint on the ground. It was a good thing these were automatic. All you needed was to compare it to the chart on the back of the bottle.

The strip turned blue.

'Jeepers!' Erina exclaimed.

She pulled out the not-sword from the sheath, holding it defensively, and scanned the forest.

It didn't feel any different. There were still small birds chirping somewhere in the canopy. Something like a squirrel climbed swiftly and disappeared into a hollow. Just normal, woodsy smells too.

Erina tried to breathe normally, but, in her chest, her heart felt like it was preparing for the worst, twisting her insides into unpleasant mush. Her muscles tensed.

The tracks were recent. *Very* recent. Whatever had made them must still be around here. But she couldn't see anything. She couldn't hear anything either. That didn't mean it wasn't watching.

A frown crept in between her eyebrows.

'You cunning bugger,' Erina breathed out. 'You circled around us, didn't you?'

Then, why wasn't Harlan freaking out? The equine had no love for iron wolves or anything else with huge fangs that thought horse was a yummy start to the day.

Sniffing the air, Erina turned against the wind. 'So, there's only one direction you *can* be, isn't there?' she muttered darkly under her breath. 'Well, I for one ain't *anyone's* lunch!'

She tightened the bags thrown over the trias' shoulders. 'Stay here Harlie. D'you hear me? Stay!'

The equine joker fidgeted, moving nervously in place. The reins thrown over his neck swung wildly.

'Where did Mordjen go, anyway?' Erina wondered, sparing a glance to the side.

From up ahead, there came a deep growl. Something large and heavy pushed the mere saplings aside. Its jaws agape, the iron wolf attacked.

It would have been better for it if it hadn't. Leaping up, catching your prey from above and crushing its back with your weight and your fangs in its neck was a great tactic when hunting swamp deer.

Erina wasn't a deer. She didn't whirl around, eyes wide. She didn't run. And with greater force then she could have ever mustered herself, the iron wolf fell onto her not-sword, impaling itself on the plastasteele.

Rolling out of the way as the grey body came crashing down on top of her, Erina narrowly avoided getting squashed.

'Well, wasn't that convenient,' she muttered as she brushed herself off. 'If I didn't know better, I'd say someone's been trying to kill me. Well, take that!' The blade had, in a million to one chance, pierced the wolf's heart.

'Good news; I ain't dead. Bad news; exactly *how* am I supposed to use a not-sword when it's stuck under several hundred kilos of dead wolf?'

Erina sighed, shaking her head at it all. 'This world really has it in for me, doesn't it?'

'And where have you been, may I ask?' She directed that last to Mordjen, who'd chosen to sneak back, on silent hooves.

He had blood around his muzzle.

'Never mind. I don't want to know, right?'

She pushed against the huge body. The fur felt coarse under her fingers. 'Guess they don't just *look* like they're made of iron. They darn right feel like it too.' She strained, putting every ounce of strength into it. It didn't budge. Not even an inch.

'Now, how am I supposed to get that back?' Erina wiped her brow. 'I don't know if anyone's listening, but I'm *not* facing a pack of angry, horse-sized beasties with teeth the size of drink bottles and breath that stinks like a three-thousand-year old unwashed armpit, with nothing but a couple of knives and Harlan's speed going for me.'

Mordjen snorted.

'Okay, and this fellow here's fangs,' she threw a thumb in the blue stallion's direction. 'So give me back my not-sword.'

It took several vines, a fair bit of ingenuity and both Mordjen's and Harlan's strength to turn the wolf on its side. And then they needed to repeat it all over again but the other way around, when the not-sword turned out to have become lodged in the ribcage because of the shift.

When Erina finally swung back up on Harlan, she collected the reins.

'I can't believe the weird in this place. Come on. The rest of the pack can't be that far ahead. We might still be able to catch them.'

Exactly what they should do if they did. Well, she hadn't quite worked out that bit … yet.

The trail soon turned. It wasn't heading into the deep forest at all. Now it was swinging outwards again and, a few hours later, the forest turned into a sparse scattering of young spruces and birch trees.

They were back on the plains again. Further north than they'd ever gone before, judging by the position of the spire of Snowfell.

'Useful mountain, that one,' Erina said. 'You always know where you are with that around. Of course, if it *hadn't* been around, I wouldn't have crashed in this weird place to begin with. Thanks for that,' she snorted.

The breeze pricked her skin. Was it just her, or was it getting colder?

'Anyone see any signs of wolves?' Erina asked. 'They can't just have disappeared.'

She couldn't make out any tracks on the ground. The supple grass before them was as tall as her knees and whatever had come through here, it had walked right over it and the supple stems had just sprung back up again behind them. Perfect camouflage. No, cover-up. No, that still wasn't quite right.

Erina bit her lip. Now wasn't the time to get hung up over a lack of words.

'Go on then,' she motioned to Mordjen who was sniffing around already. 'You're a big, bad predator. I'm sure your nose is a lot more useful than my eyes right now.'

Question now was, how far ahead were they? And would they find them first?

Then Mordjen snorted, an almost yip, yip sound from between pointed teeth and took off.

'Finally,' Erina exclaimed. 'Yah! Harlan. Yah!'

The trias collected his legs, bunched up, and practically leapt forward as her legs squeezed his barrel to keep from falling off.

They surged forth like an unstoppable tide rolling in after the equinox. For a moment, they ran almost side by side. Running, muscles moving under sweating bodies, carrying them faster and faster. Manes streamed in the wind. The heavy breath of exertion blowing rhythmically between them.

Mordjen almost seemed to fly, his hooves barely touching the ground. The light, supple motions of a predator; dark, almost black, against the cerulean sky.

Above them, the suns were basking down unforgivingly, as if it was the height of summer rather than mere spring. From up on high, they watched the two equines race.

Harlan and Mordjen. Their hooves thundered against the hard earth. In unison, yet different, they existed together in nothing but that brief moment of time just then. One leaping, the other pounding the ground with sharp hooves. One surging ahead, his head held high, his mane whipping Erina in the face. Stinging her. The other, his head forwards, lips parted and curled with a trace of white glinting between them.

Over stock and stone they went. They scared up birds hiding amongst the tall grasses. Amongst the reeds. Sent rabbits fleeing for their burrows. Flew over ditches and old streambeds.

Erina clung tightly to her mount. Her legs didn't ache anymore, but the air stung her eyes from the dust at this speed. They grew misty and wet, tears of irritation leaking from them.

Clutching tightly to a bunch of his mane, she held on tightly to the reins. Not that they'd do her much good right now. Harlan had eyes only for the other horse. Right now, everything else was forgotten. Even the wolves they were supposed to be chasing. All he could see was Mordjen. Mordjen up front, where *he* should be.

As the dark blue horse crested the hill they'd been climbing, he let out a fierce cry. Leaping almost straight out from the top of the hill, the skeletal stumps on his sides snapped open. They spread out, almost like wings. Wings without membranes.

There was no way he should have been able to fly. But, in between, where stretched skin should have been, something shimmered. Like a dark promise, shadow and light, together, warped space and sight between them.

Mordjen dove down the steep hill. Downwards he went. Downwards, towards the pack.

She could hear them now, long before they surged over the hill and charged into the fray themselves. The yaps. The snarls.

This time, Harlan didn't hesitate. Adrenaline surged through his body, pumping courage into his heart. His legs carried him, without stopping, over the top of the hill and down into the sunken depression beyond.

The iron wolves were waiting.

The world turned into chaos as the horse and rider smacked right into the fray. Howls and barks and angry screams. The smell of damp dust and earth mingled with the iron scent of warm blood.

Then they were through. Careening through a small copse, the wet leaves slapped Erina in the face. Now the wolves were on *their* trail. Harlan kept running. He swerved around the obstacles, narrowly avoiding unseating her.

Behind them came noise. The sound of heavy paws upon the earth. Of breaking trees. Crushed opposition.

They were even larger when all seen together. Hackles raised, chests puffed out.

The growls, rising and falling in pitch. It did strange things to your insides. To your senses.

Heavy on their feet, they were putting on a fair turn of speed, especially considering they were having to run through some pretty tough brambles.

Harlan ran faster, slipping through spaces a larger body should have struggled with. *They* merely pushed them aside. Tore them asunder.

Erina gritted her teeth and wished she had a blaster. Or something big and heavy that went "kabloom" and turned whatever you aimed it at into very small pieces indeed[11] along with a significant portion of the surroundings.

Of course, with those it was usually considered a good idea to be far away

---

[11] Thereby also ceasing to bother you. Though some beings could be very vindictive and, even after scattering them into a cloud formation, the last thing you wanted was to breathe them in.

from whatever you attempted to blow up. *Very* far away if they were concussion torpedoes. Also, it helped if you were a starship, not a heredrome sprinting through an arboreal retreat.

Bursting out of the copse at speed, Harlan veered sharply. Now they plunged right into their pursuers. It became a churning cauldron of thrashing limbs. A set of fangs flashed before her eyes.

Erina didn't have many memories of the next five minutes. The screams came as though from a distance, as if she heard them through twenty feet of water. As if what was happening wasn't happening to her. Red became the state of her mind. And as instincts took over, red flowed down her blade.

The pack had them outnumbered. Outmanoeuvred. The battle *should* have been one-sided — or, at the very least, more one-sided than it was. The combatants kicked, squealed, and slashed with their claws, fangs, hooves, and steel.

An iron wolf went down.

Still they fought. Fought with the fury of those that knew they had nowhere to run. Nowhere to hide.

It was hard to say what changed. Maybe it was something in the wind. Some scent drifting in, meandering, percolating slowly through the Valley. But as Erina's grip tightened around the hilt of her not-sword, tensing for their next attack, the iron wolves — the huge, hulking brutes that they were — whimpered. Their stone-encrusted ears drooped.

Then, one by one, they cowered back. Then, one whined, broke rank and made a run for it. Yipping and whining, the rest of the pack turned and followed.

'And STAY out!' Erina shouted after the few retreating iron wolves.

The world stopped spinning for her. Like waking up from a daze, she tasted something warm and sticky in her mouth and running down her face.

Realizing she was only seeing out of one eye, she rubbed the blood off. There, that was better.

'Wonder what scared them so?' she cast both eyes around, but there was nothing there. At least, nothing that should have frightened such formidable opponents.

And, as the large, dark grey bodies disappeared in the distance all the adrenaline was making her ears tingle now that it was no longer having to deal with things trying to gnaw her into little pieces.

'Good riddance,' she breathed, rubbing her hands on the stained trousers. The world, which had been foggy and difficult to grasp, slowed down to meet her. Her legs were shaking from all that spent energy.

'Everyone alive?' Erina checked the only moving bodies within range.

Mordjen leapt forward. Every muscle quivered with tension. Like a rach defending its den, he screamed defiance at the departing pack. It was doubtful they could run any faster, yapping and whining as they went.

'Well, someone's not out of energy it seems.'

Whirling on the spot, the air between the skeletal stumps on his withers shimmered, almost lifting him from the ground. Back and forth Mordjen loped. Stopping dramatically. Sniffing at a dead body. Snorting and, with a start, off he was again. His chest and barrel was heaving, but it took time for him to settle down.

'Guess I don't need to ask if he's got any troubles,' Erina shook her head at the strange equine's behaviour. She could see he'd been injured, but it didn't look like it was anything that bothered him too much. Maybe when the adrenaline wore off, it'd be a different matter.

Harlan trotted over to her where she'd slumped on the ground and snuffled into her blood-soaked hair, snorting at the distasteful scent.

'Yeah, I need a bath, I know. Heck, I need three. Still in one piece?' She rubbed at his forehead.

For all the cuts and scrapes and far too close encounters with huge, yellow teeth, the trias seemed to have come out of the whole event with only minor injuries.

There was matted blood covering parts of his coat, but, judging by the smell and the colour, it wasn't his. Something to be grateful for, then. There *were* bitemarks along his neck, but, on closer inspection, they didn't look deep and, with a bit of cleaning, they should heal.

'Are we supposed to do something with this?' Erina wondered, aiming a small kick at the nearest furry body. The only thing that accomplished was adding a stubbed toe to the list of injuries.

'The fur might be handy, but do any of *you* know how to skin something like this?'

Now that she could see them up close, and had time to take a closer look without them trying to tear her throat out, it was hard to believe anyone would actually fight one of these things voluntarily — to say nothing about a whole pack. What had she been thinking?

Hugely muscular, they were covered in fur that shifted from being coarse to something more akin to spikes than hair around the neck. Their paws were huge, far larger than you'd have expected even considering the iron wolves' size and with traces of webbing between the toes (she discovered after a bit of poking).

There were hard protrusions rising from the elbows up over the shoulders, parting the fur as they clustered together. These could be seen knotting themselves together over the eyes as well, forming a solid, hard forehead devoid of anything.

The fur itself disappeared about half-way down the animals' legs and, while craggy on their backs, there was almost none descending below their underbellies.

'Whatever these things are, they're not from around here,' Erina declared.

She looked over the area where the battle had brought them. It was beginning to smell already. The open plain had shrunk and was now being flanked by either forest climbing upwards a distant mountain range or ochre-coloured cliffs that had seen better days.

'How far away from shuttlehome are we, anyway?' she asked the world. 'I don't recognize any of this.'

She could never get over how distances in the Valley were never what you expected them to be. One day, it took you two hours to reach the nearest stream and the next, the same amount of time brought you high into the mountains.

Whatever was behind it, it certainly wasn't obeying any scientific laws she knew about. But she was getting used to the strangeness of it all. It was odd, but in a kind of expected way. If that made sense.

Had she always felt like that? Erina tried to shake the blood out of her hair. Her ears were whistling. Her eyes swimming.

Retreating from the battlefield, they rested just beyond the hill. Then, gathering up her two companions, Erina decided to leave the slain wolves behind. She didn't really know what to do with them and there was no real way to bring them back with them.

Besides, not even Mordjen was eating them. He'd taken a few experimental nips, but, aside from managing to make a face of disgust, he'd let them be after that.

'No. If even he doesn't want them, I'm certainly not going to. Food poisoning is bad enough once. Let's not go there again, shall we?'

Straightening the remains of Harlan's halter, Erina pulled herself onto the horse's back. 'Hupp!'

It was as they headed out after resting, turning towards home, that a light in the corner of her eyes made her look up. And then up again.

High upon the broken, ochre crags, something shimmered. Something almost equine, alight like the sun, blazed so bright she had to avert her eyes. The warmth washed over her, even from this distance. She had to shield her face from the heat of a thousand furnaces.

When she dared open her eyes again, it was gone.

'What the...? What was that? Another mystery. Why not. Just add them to the pile. I seem to be hoarding them lately, anyway.'

Beneath her, Harlan fidgeted at the annoyed hisses coming from her lips. She nudged him forwards and he took off at a brisk trot.

'Ouch, ouch, ouch,' Erina cried out. 'Not so fast, Harlie. Slow down. I'm not in *that* much of a hurry to check it out!'

Meanwhile, Mordjen flowed in circles around them as they headed towards the bottom of the crags where the mysterious apparition had appeared.

It took a while to find a way up; the crags themselves being just several levels of sheer drops when you looked up, but around, on the other side, they sloped down. It was steep, but you could climb it, even if you were a horse.

A lot of effort later, and Erina shaded her eyes again. This time from the suns. The top of the crags offered excellent views, but today she wasn't sure what she was looking at.

'Oh, boy,' she said. 'What a mess. How the heck did we miss this?'

The shuttle, having partially disintegrated in flight, had strewn parts (some even recognizable, had she been an engineer) all along its so-not-stable descent path.

'Okay, so crash path would be more accurate, but who's ever heard of that? It wasn't like we were doing much flying towards the end. I guess I should be happy it's not bits of me scattered all over the place,' she entrusted to Harlan. 'That would be messier. Although, I suppose, there'd be no remains left by now. Unlike me, space stuff isn't exactly biodegradable.'

Maybe that was what was wrong with the picture, she mused. The plastasteele and its ilk would stay like they were, practically forever. Sure, things might eventually start burying them or begin growing on them, but the inner part, the heart of it, would remain down the ages.

'Someone really should do something about that.' She followed up with a huge sigh and shrug when the realization dawned that the only one around to do anything about it was her.

'Bother,' she said.

She gave the diom around her wrist a small shake. She wasn't sure why she still carried the thing around. It wasn't like it was of any use here.

'You're supposed to be able to pick up a signal from these things through several kilometres of rock, but here you just plain refuse to operate? Sure, passing through a star might be troublesome and I suppose a black hole would eat you for breakfast, but there's nothing here, *nothing* between you and the bloody satellites in orbit but sky, sky, sky and a cloud or two?'

Of the golden shimmer there was no trace. Not a stray piece of fluff. Not even a footprint. And with the heat it had been emitting, it should have melted the crag into slag.

'You've got some seriously strange neighbours Harlie,' Erina told the horse.

It took several days to return to familiar surroundings. When Erina finally pulled back on the makeshift halter, a few stones, kicked loose by hard hooves, began tumbling their way down from up on high.

Harlan stopped with a snort. Pawing at the stony ground of the hill they'd just climbed, he wanted to go on — move on — despite his sides heaving with the exertion of getting them both to the top.

'Easy there, boy,' Erina said. 'You'll get to run soon enough, run to your heart's content. Just wait a bit, okay.'

She patted his arched muscular neck. Harlan tried to prance, remembered how precariously he stood, and thought better of it.

'This place, it sure is just a little bit bigger than I expected,' Erina confided in him.

It was difficult to tell if it was reverential or not. Most of what she said was like that. Probably why most humans tended to misunderstand her a lot.

Harlan was different. This place was different. Erina wasn't the naturalistic type, but there was something about here that called to the very bones in her body — now that she'd stopped trying to drown out the sensation.

Mordjen, who heaved himself up the last part of the steep incline to stand beside them, regarded them solemnly. His serpentine tails moved cautiously as the spiked blue wonder tossed his head in the warm spring breeze.

'For better or worse, this is our world now. Harlan. Mordjen.' Erina murmured softly.

Beneath them, in the distance, there was a glint, as if from something metallic. Shuttlehome.

'We really should give this place a name you know?' Erina bit at a finger.

They watched the shadows and light play across the landscape as above them fluffy clouds chased each other across the sky.

'Shadows and light. That's what this place is. One moment it's one thing, the next another. Yes, shadows and light. Light and shadow. Hmm … Darkness. Darklight. Darklight Valley. Yes. Darklight Valley it is.'

Erina tasted the words as they rolled over her tongue. They felt right … somehow.

Whatever things would come next, the one thing she was certain of was that it wouldn't be anything at all like her old life.

'Not quite the type of adventure I was looking for. Could be worse, I suppose. But I'm still finding a way out of here, d'you hear!?' she called out into the wind.

Erina nudged the stallion's sides lightly with her heels and the horse, that magnificent, impossible creation of the wind, leapt forward, carrying them all into the future.

Something … watched them go.

THE END?

Acknowledgements

High Fyelds' journey started many, many moons ago now, long before it was even called High Fyelds. In light of that, I'd like to thank HARPG for many years of fun and laughter and general shenanigans.

FlyingGekko once again chose to trust me with one of her characters via the "create your own character tier" at the time of the launch of "The Damsel and the Dragon" and I hope you all like him. Mordjen is a sweetie, even if you'd probably run very far, very fast, if you ever met him in a dark alley ;-)

Again, a huge thanks goes out to my cover artist, Juliane Völker, who valiantly took on the challenge of drawing horses, instead of the dragons we both love and adore, for both of the first "High Fyelds" books.

And an ever huger thanks (and extra huggles) for my brilliant editor, Ashley Lachance for putting up with me. I'm so sorry for all the horrible comma gremlins and their ilk that I subjected you to in this manuscript. I swear they multiply when I'm not looking.

Equal thanks go to my wonderful readers, Wanda Aasen, Lark Cunningham, Aramanth Dawe, Elizabeth-Rose Best, Skywings14, Tyler Richter, Ashli T, Tasha Turner, Scott Schaper, Rhonda Harms and Rhel ná DecVandé, who helped launch this out into the world. This wouldn't be nearly as fun without you all :)

I should probably thank the Muse too. The Little Darling has been bombarding me with ideas for future books even as I was trying to finish-up this one.

Chrono-order of the Seven of Stars Novels

Seven of Stars isn't written chronologically (you can blame the Muse for that), so if you'd like to read the books in the order they actually take place within their universe, this won't be the order in which they were published. The good thing is, you don't *need* to read them in any particular order to enjoy them.

The universe itself is divided into seven different **Ages**.

1st Age -3rd Age

4th Age
"The Damsel and the Dragon"
"Magical Mischief"
"You're a Dragon" (coming in 2018)

5th Age
"The Dawn of the Winds"
"Wolf's Bane"

6th Age
"The Soul Within" (coming 2019)
"High Fyelds – A New Beginning"
"High Fyelds – The Big Race"

7th Age
"Academia Draconia"

AD

HIGH FYELDS

THE BIG RACE

Deciding the enter Harlan - her quick-footed jester stallion - into a prestegious race, Erina is thrown into the cutthroat world of natural racing.

But when you race against nightmares, it brings a whole new meaning to the competition wanting to take a bite out of the action.

Mae McKinnon

 DragonQuill Publishing

Scribe Cat

Helping writers create clear, concise, and credible work!

We hope you enjoyed *High Fyelds!*

This book was made possible with the help of an Editor.

A professional edit is an invaluable resource in preparing a manuscript for print, whether that means sewing up plot holes, tidying up runaway sentences, or catching the last few typos.

With over 10 years of experience, Ashley Lachance has worked with authors to prepare novels, short stories, magazine articles, and academic writing for publication. Regardless of length, genre, or stage of development, your project deserves a skillful revision.

Have a story or manuscript waiting for a second pair of eyes?

What are you waiting for? Don't pro-cat-stinate!

Check out ScribeCat.ca and get a free quote today!

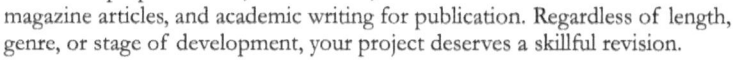

🌐 www.ScribeCat.ca

✉ ashley@ScribeCat.ca

🐦 @Scribe_Cat

f facebook.com/ScribeCat

The Damsel and the Dragon

Or so the sages say. Linandra isn't so sure.

Maybe that's because, unlike most sages', Lin's life actually contains dragons. Several of them.

But they don't cause anywhere near as much trouble as the wizards, mages, sorcerers and other arcane users that inhabits her new home.

Welcome to the Twin Towers.

Mae McKinnon

DragonQuill Publishing

Do YOU have what it takes to face your fears?

THEN JOIN THE DRAGONCORPS
AND PROTECT THE SKIES
OF NEW RETMIA!

Academia Draconia

The school where courage matters!

For Gaile Ashworthey and her fellow students, getting into the Dragon Research Centre had been easy.

. The hard part was staying long enough to graduate.

Trouble is, Gaile has a terrible head for heights. Not to mention, she's not big on teamwork.

But teamwork is what a dragon and rider is all about. If she's going to find a partner, it's going to take a dragon unlike any other.

Mae McKinnon

 DRAGONQUILL PUBLISHING

THE SOUL WITHIN

What they want is a superweapon.
What they need is a miracle.
What they get...

Earth's cities lie abandoned. The people that remain live in vast, subterranean vaults; the last refuges of human kind.

With resources running out, the battle against the alien invaders is periously close to failing.

In this world, a child and a machine dream of soaring through the sky.

COMING 2019

Mae McKinnon

DRAGONQUILL PUBLISHING

www.ingramcontent.com/pod-product-compliance
Lightning Source LLC
Chambersburg PA
CBHW020320130626
46549CB00003B/947